Steve Wilhelm's: Another Time To Love

Another Time To Love

By: Steve Wilhelm

Copyright © 2017 Steve Wilhelm

Cover design by Jessica Ozment

This is a work of fiction. Any similarities persons, alive or dead, are purely coincidental. No part of this book can be reproduced in any form without the expressed written consent by the author.

Steve Wilhelm's: Another Time To Love

Acknowledgements

I am grateful to Nikki Strycharz not only for being such a wonderful fan, but she's been a huge inspiration to me and my writing. I thank Nikki for being my sounding board, my BETA reader and my friend.

Thank you to Jessica Tahbonemah for her wickedly awesome cover work. She makes things pop out and catch your eye!! Thank you also, Jessica for assisting with grammar, continuity and making sure the book reads well.

Thank you to Heidi Boden for always being there for me. Love you!

A special thank you to all of my readers. I write for you!!

Steve Wilhelm's: Another Time To Love

Dedication

To Nikki.

Steve Wilhelm's: Another Time To Love

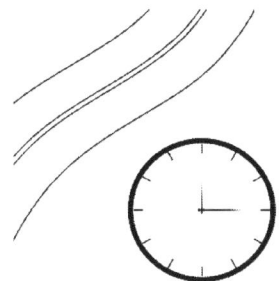

CHAPTER ONE

I sat up in bed with a start and opened my eyes. As my vision adjusted and I could better see my surroundings, I relaxed slightly and lowered myself back into a more comfortable position. What a freaky dream that was, I thought as I glanced around the bedroom Betty and I shared for over fifteen years. I closed my eyes once again and stretched, enjoying the sensation as I loosened my tired and aching muscles. The image of seeing me on the bed in the dark, cold warehouse with Jules and Maggie standing over me, thankfully was fading. How bizarre was it that I had the dream to begin with? Amazing how realistic dreams can be, I thought.

    This one, had been so real that I think it may be a good idea to re-think my decision to meet with Mathew, today, or any day. God forbid if I ever tampered with my destiny by doing what I did in the dream; so much damage to have to live with. How I got myself so worked up

Steve Wilhelm's: Another Time To Love

because I didn't know what happened to Jules way back then, I really have no clue. Life is good. I don't need to take for granted what I have and where I am!

I tottered out of bed and carried myself into the bathroom to turn on the water in the shower. After it ran sufficiently hot, I stepped in and closed the sliding glass door. Once I was ready, I reached for my shampoo and noticed Betty must have changed from her usual brand. In its place, was an herbal formula with a sweet strawberry scent. I've smelled this before, I thought. How long has Betty been using this?

I finished up and rinsed myself off, almost ready to start the day. I stepped out of the shower and picked the bath towel up off the counter. After drying off, I started to put the towel in the hamper and looked closely at the color of the fabric. I ran a hand over the soft blue material with ease. Curious, I thought, I could have sworn we had dark-green towels. I opened the closet next to the door and spotted that every single one was the same color, blue. What was going on? Maybe I was coming down with a case of senility. I laughed out loud at the idea. I've been working too hard. It was a wise decision to take the week off, as I had.

In the kitchen, I pulled down the coffee bin with my favorite dark Columbian Roast coffee from *Costco*. I got out the filters and then looked at the coffee pot. What the hell? Not only was there a half pot of coffee left in the carafe, but as I felt the side, it was still warm. Was I truly going mad? Maybe I got up earlier, drank some and then

Steve Wilhelm's: Another Time To Love

went back to bed? It wasn't inconceivable, I'd done it before.

I filled a mug and put it in the microwave and watched the digital numbers tick down until it was done. I pulled the hot cup out and retrieved the creamer from the fridge. Just as I was topping off my coffee cup, the door kitchen's garage door opened and I saw Megan come in carrying two overfull sacks of groceries in both her arms. It startled me so much that I dropped the creamer to the floor with a crash. She froze, letting out a shriek before dropping her own bags from her arms and then quickly approached with her hands out in self-defense. She suddenly recognized me and stopped mid-stance, with a look of fear that shifted into surprise and caring concern.

"Daddy?"

"Megan?" I said when I found my voice. "What are you doing here?"

"Daddy? You're awake? Oh, my God," her voice rose in excitement. "What are you out of bed? You okay?" She rushed over to me and took me in her arms, hugging me in a tight embrace.

"Honey, what's going on? Shouldn't you be with Mom at school? You know, Parent's Week?" I was beyond confused. There were weird things happening ever since I got out of bed.

"You don't remember much, do you Daddy?" Megan pulled back slightly and looked at me with her wide open eyes. "We repeatedly called you for two days,

Steve Wilhelm's: Another Time To Love

and you weren't answering, so Mom and I booked the next available flight back."

"What? Megan, I don't understand," I said warily as I examined her face for any sign of a prank. She and Betty were no strangers to practical jokes, many of which had us complaining of stomach cramps from laughing too hard. There was no indication of anything close to a ruse.

"Why are you calling me Megan?" She asked, equally perplexed.

"What do you mean? That's your name, honey," I answered. "Ever since you were born."

"I'm Maggie, you goof!" She laughed uncertainly. "Anyway, so Mom and I came home and found you on the living room floor, delirious and burning up with fever. You've been sleeping for three days straight, basically ever since we got home."

"Well that's kind of crazy, don't you think? I mean, seriously, last night I was just out at the—" I paused abruptly, something was not right. How could I have been asleep when I was discussing with Mathew about how he could help me remember Jules. I know it was last evening!! What was Maggie talking about? "Are you guys pulling one over on me? Where's Mom?" I bent over to collect the groceries that were all over the kitchen floor and suddenly a powerful wave of nausea washed over me. My head started pounding and I ended up sitting with my back to the stove. My forehead was suddenly damp with beads of sweat.

Steve Wilhelm's: Another Time To Love

"You should be in bed, Daddy," Maggie said as she grabbed the towel off the stove handle and gingerly wiped my brow. "You shouldn't be rushing things, you know? Don't worry about the mess in here, I'll take care of it, but we need to get you back to bed."

I couldn't really disagree with her reasoning. I seriously had no idea what was wrong with me, but I was quite certain it was kicking the shit out of me. "Where's Mom," I inquired again as I slowly got to my feet with her help.

"She'll be home soon, don't worry," Maggie answered dotingly. "But I'm afraid she'll give us both the riot act if anything were to happen to you on my watch!"

"I'm not sure, but I think it might be too late for that," I mumbled more to myself than to my daughter as she half carried me up the stairs and down the hall back to the bedroom.

"What's that Daddy? I couldn't really understand you," she said between grunts. My little girl wasn't used to helping her dad in this way.

"Nothing honey," I lied. My vision was blurring in and out of focus and I was seeing things everywhere that were no longer familiar. Some of the pictures hanging in the hallway were fine, but there was one that caught my eye as I passed it. It was Maggie, me and . . . Jules? Sitting on the porch of the cabin we used to go to some summers. That's not right, not at all. More like impossible. Maybe it was my fevered mind playing tricks on me, but the wallpaper looked different! Even the carpet didn't

Steve Wilhelm's: Another Time To Love

appear to be the right color, or texture. I never noticed these things as I had wandered to the kitchen just a little earlier.

I could barely keep my eyes open as Maggie helped me into bed. I didn't have the energy to undress anything and I wasn't about to ask Maggie to do it for me. I just needed a little more sleep, and then when I wake up again, everything is going to be back to normal. At least that's what I hoped. She pulled the blanket up to my chin, leaning over to gently kiss my cheek.

"Get some more rest, Daddy," she cooed. "We'll check on you again as soon as Mom gets home. She'll be really glad to know you are okay now. Well, at least out of your sleep anyway."

I was beginning to think that I was nowhere close to being grounded, and that far worse things were just around the corner. I heard Maggie turn out the lights and then darkness enveloped the room.

Steve Wilhelm's: Another Time To Love

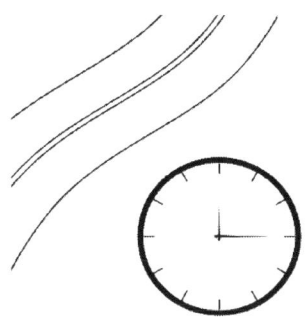

CHAPTER TWO

Somewhere in the distance, I could hear Maggie's amplified voice. "See Mom, his eyes are moving, I think Daddy's waking up again," she sounded enthusiastic. "I'll go get some ice water, I'm sure he'll be thirsty."

I heard footsteps traveling from the room, and then a cool damp cloth was on my forehead. It felt good and I moaned slightly as I attempted to open my eyes. I needed to see my precious wife who's finally here to take care of me.

"Betty?" I managed weakly, my voice barely a whisper. The movement with the cloth on my head suddenly stopped.

"Danny?" Only one person ever called me by that name.

Steve Wilhelm's: Another Time To Love

"Why are you calling me Betty?" I was asked. "Maggie told me you called her a different name earlier, too."

I opened my eyes. Jules' worried face filled my sight. I must have cringed somewhat. "Jules?" I croaked.

"Well this is a first, my darling. I've never actually seen you pull away from me in all our time together. I'm thinking we should probably call the doctor to make a house call, because you seriously don't look well." She gently stroked my damp hair a few times.

"No, I— I just wasn't expecting . . ." I didn't know how to finish my own explanation.

"Danny, what's wrong? You look like you've seen a ghost. Your face is so pale!"

Was this still a dream? Was Jules real? So many thoughts paraded around in my head that I couldn't trust anything I might say in response. It wasn't that I was seeing a ghost, because she was here. In the flesh, but how could she be here? Last I knew, she had disappeared sometime after high school graduation. Somehow though, she's right here and she and I are married? I reached out and gingerly touched Jules' quivering shoulder. "Jules?" I whispered again. She looked at me, her eyes in open confusion.

"What is wrong with you? Has that fever done something to your brain, Daniel? You're clearly not yourself."

Suddenly a barrage of images flashed before my unfocused eyes. It was as if I was about to die and my life

Steve Wilhelm's: Another Time To Love

was playing out as a tribute to my existence. I saw my meeting with Mathew. I saw myself undergoing his treatment and him sending me back to my past; Jules and I going to Reno and getting married. I even saw her disappear after we returned. There was college and meeting Betty, dating and going steady. Mom dying, Jules showing up out of the blue after the services, and meeting my daughter. Unfortunately, I wasn't saved from also experiencing when I chose Jules over Betty, or seeing Jules dye after that mugging and me raising Maggie all by myself. I saw myself reuniting with Betty and us getting married. I saw this in a manner of seconds, even though it was virtually half a lifetime.

"You're . . . you're not dead," I choked out the last word and reached for her, clutching her body to mine in a tight embrace. I kissed her neck and inhaled the scent of strawberries in her soft hair. She hugged me back and then finally, I sat up and held my hands to her beating heart.

"No, of course I'm not dead," she answered apprehensively. "Feel my heartbeat, if you don't believe me."

There it was, I felt it thumping strong and steady. Shivers ran up and down my spine, forcing an involuntary shake. I didn't know what to think anymore. I smiled and tears filled my confused eyes. I forcefully blinked several times before Jules leaned in and kissed the tears away.

"I've really missed you, Jules, you have no idea," I said and brought her lips to mine. I began to kiss her,

Steve Wilhelm's: Another Time To Love

timid at first. It felt for a moment that she was going to pull away, then she opened her mouth and our tongues danced together. I could feel her heartbeat race, and warmth filled my body as it responded to her closeness. After a moment of enjoying our unbridled fervor, we finally parted.

"Wow, Danny," she breathed heavily, her face flush. "You haven't kissed me like that in a very long time."

"It seems like forever," I agreed.

"Can you tell me what's going on inside that head of yours? You seem different," she questioned as she took her fingers and caressed my cheek. "Not a bad different, but . . . you know. Kind of like way back when."

"Way back when?" I inquired.

"Yes," Jules' eyes grew distant for a moment. "It was right after graduation. Remember, I came over for breakfast with you and your Mom and it just seemed like you were a different person then, so full of wonder and life. I mean, more than the day before, but your mom noticed it, too!"

I remembered it, just like she had. That was the morning after I first went back. Everything was so new to me, it had been all I could do to keep myself together and not let on I wasn't exactly the same Daniel she knew, but something obviously had gone awry. The present outcome was altered from what I recalled when I woke up earlier. I needed time to think about my situation before I said anything else to anyone. Who knows, more could

Steve Wilhelm's: Another Time To Love

have changed. I seem to have royally pissed off someone in the Destiny department and now I'm being paid in full for my decisions.

"Jules, I honestly don't know how to explain anything to you about me and what's going on," I clarified. "But what I do know, is that I feel better than I did when I first woke up."

"Do you know why you called Maggie Megan?"

"No," I said. I didn't like to lie, but what was the alternative? "And why I called you Betty? I know that's on your mind, too. I don't have anything to offer there either. I think I just need to rest some more to get rid of this incessant headache that's been with me ever since I woke up this morning."

Maggie came in the room with a tall glass of ice water with a straw sticking out of it. She looked rather tense but when she saw Jules and I smiling at each other, she visibly relaxed and smiled herself. "Is everything okay now?" Maggie asked.

"Well, as okay as it can be at the moment," Jules told her. "I think we should leave Dad to rest some more and see how he is tonight."

"Maybe we can all have dinner together," Maggie suggested. "Do you think you'll have an appetite by then Daddy?"

"Anything is possible sweetie," I said and yawned. "Let me have some of that ice water though, would you?" Maggie brought the glass over and angled the straw towards my mouth. I certainly could have handled the

15

Steve Wilhelm's: Another Time To Love

task of drinking by myself, but I let Maggie be the nurse. I swallowed almost half of the glass before gently pushing it away. The water was so good and soothing as it went down. I hadn't realized how thirsty I was.

No matter how hard I tried, or how tired I was, I was still unable to get my rest. I couldn't find a comfortable position to even begin to relax. My brain was spinning with an information overload that began this morning when I greeted the day. Finally, I gave up and laid back to stare at the ceiling. I cleared my mind as best I could and tried to process what was happening to me.

It's amazing how something so innocent could explode and snowball into a complicated, life-altering path that had no sides and nothing to hold on to. All I had intended to do was find out about a part of my past that I couldn't remember. I didn't expect the ripple effect of changes that resulted in my altered life. To be fair, it wasn't just my life, but similarly everyone associated with me has been affected, to some extent, be it a better end, or a worse. How many alterations had I caused? I've already noted a handful since this morning, but that could very well be only the tip of the iceberg.

I'll probably decide the best thing I can do, more than anything else, is to just accept things for what they are. I did that the last time when Jeff and I failed every attempt to get me back to my original body. It's okay, I thought it was the right thing to do. When Jules came back into my life after she disappeared, I think Destiny

Steve Wilhelm's: Another Time To Love

was doing its best to revert events back to the way they were supposed be. Especially when Jules was killed during the mugging. I'm not so sure anymore, the rules seemed to have changed. I've obviously done something else to somehow cause even more ripples in my timeline. All I know, is nothing at all is the same as yesterday. Jules is alive? How can that be? It's all too much to comprehend. I needed my brain to stop rambling and give me some peace!

    I got up out of bed and found some ibuprofen in the bathroom cabinet. Without caring about the dosage, I swallowed five pills, guzzling down my water bottle so that I could stare at myself in the mirror. Was this really me? It appears I have grey hair now, though I can't remember noticing that before. Jesus, there are certainly some major stress lines in my forehead that I don't recall ever being there. I stretched the skin to smooth out the wrinkles, but they came right back when I let go of the slack. If this is the worst I can find that's happened, then I should probably count my blessings.

    I stretched out on the bed once more. I really need to talk to someone about things. Not Jules, only because I know she would not understand. Besides, I didn't want her to have to think about the fact that she's essentially back from the dead. Though I'm quite certain most anyone would be freaked out about that sort of detail.

    Well, maybe not Jeff. He's pretty much the most pragmatic guy I know. I wasn't sure at first, if he would believe me, the last time I opened to him about being

Steve Wilhelm's: Another Time To Love

from the future, he surprised me. Of course, he has always believed in me and had my back from day one. I can't remember him ever not being my best friend. I smiled to myself and breathed a bit easier. Yes, I needed to talk with Jeff. I convinced him once before, I can convince him again. Doubt entered my mind suddenly and a wave of fear creeped over me. "What if another result of whatever I have recently done has caused him to change as well? What if he died again from that damn cancer? Or, what if he had never been a survivor to begin with?" He thought.

"I'll just have to find this out tomorrow. I've got to try not to stress out about the things I have no control over. For now, I'm going to have enough on my plate just trying to keep calm and not let on about things. I don't need anyone thinking I'm a nutcase, though if I were to see Dr. Stevens, I'm quite sure he would have me committed." I smiled.

Closing my eyes and nestling my head deep into the pillow, I began to plan my agenda of things to carry out the next day. That was my intention, until I fell fast asleep.

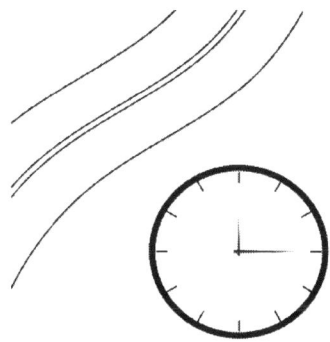

CHAPTER THREE

Jules brought a piping hot pot of coffee over and topped off my cup. I watched as the scorching nectar's steam rose into the air and disappeared as the steam reached my lips. She took my breakfast plate which formerly held eggs, bacon and hash browns and slid it over to the vacant side of the table. It was one of the best breakfasts I can remember eating. She then set the coffee pot next to my empty plate and sat in my lap, putting her arms around my neck.

"Good morning, again," I spoke, as Jules brought her full lips to mine. Her tongue sought out mine and I could sense the sweet taste of orange juice on her breath. It was truly an exhilarating way to start the day, and when

Steve Wilhelm's: Another Time To Love

she pulled her head back and licked her lips, she left me wanting much more.

"I just wanted to make sure you were awake," she assured with a grin.

"Oh, you can be sure all of me is awake," I said, slightly squirming as she had caused a growth in my pants. I think she felt it, because she started to rhythmically move her hips against me. I enjoyed the pressure she was applying and caught my breath. "Is this the normal morning routine, or are you just happy to see me?"

"Mmm . . ." Jules cooed. "I'm definitely happy to see you... and very pleased that all necessary parts are working as they were designed to. Besides, would there be anything wrong with making this a habit?" She leaned in playfully to kiss me again.

"Oh, come *on* guys! Really?" Maggie exclaimed with an upturned nose as she walked in on our moment. "I don't mean to sound cliché, but seriously, just get a room!"

"Mags, most kids don't even have two parents around, much less, both parents who are in as much love as we are. We're just expressing that affection," Jules replied coyly.

"Oh, well... sure. In public, hand holding and things like that are fine, Mom, but you're practically giving Dad a freaking lap dance!"

"Oh, geeze," I snickered, burying my face in Jules' neck in embarrassment.

"How do you think I'm doing?" Jules asks.

Steve Wilhelm's: Another Time To Love

"Actually, pretty good, Mom. You could probably get a part-time gig at the 'Vu downtown with a little more practice," Maggie said jokingly.

Jules got up and glanced at her wrist watch. "Oh shit, I've got to get going. If I'm late again, I may have to seriously consider your suggestion."

"Forgive my rattled brain Hun, but where do you work again?" I had to take any opportunity I could to learn the unknowns when I could, otherwise I was going to have a hell of a time trying to navigate this foreign landscape.

"Of course, you are forgiven, this once, Darling," Jules smiled at me sweetly. "I just finished the training and tests at D B Interior Designs, only the biggest and best in Seattle."

"You go Mom!! I'm proud of you," Maggie said and gave her a kiss on the cheek and shouldered her purse.

"Where are you off to?" Jules kissed her back.

"Since I don't go back to New York until Sunday, I thought I'd catch up with Alan."

"Who's Alan?" I asked.

"Maggie was seeing this guy on and off during the summer, don't you remember Daniel?" Jules shook her head sympathetically at my blank stare. "I'm sure all of this will come back to you soon. Anyways, she was all googly-eyed with him weren't you Maggie?" She gave Maggie a quick wink.

"Oh, Mother," the teenager rolled her eyes, almost to the point of them popping out. "We're just friends. We friend-zoned each other a while ago, so it's not really like that."

"Uh huh, well you better be careful, I see the adoration in Alan's eyes every time he looks at you." Jules looked at me and laughed good-naturedly.

"*Bye* Mom, bye Dad," she said with a smile as she went out the door.

"I'm sure we'll see her before she heads back to school," I kidded. "Hey, I have no idea if I've told you lately how proud I am of you, too. You really are a go-getter, and God help anyone who gets in your way!"

"Well, yes, you have, but honestly, I will never tire of hearing your compliments," Jules looked at me for a moment. "Danny, I just adore you!"

I squeezed her arm. "You better go, my love."

"Yes, you're right. If I stick around much longer, I might just have to take you back to bed!"

After Jules left, I heated up the rest of my coffee in the microwave and sipped at it while contemplating a few things. I stared out the kitchen window watching the hummingbirds fluttering around the feeder hanging from the tree nearby. Hummingbirds? When did we get that feeder? I shook my head. I had to marvel at the resiliency of the human spirit to adapt to even the most bizarre of situational changes. Case in point for me, that in such a brief time, I find myself falling back into the caring routines and atmosphere with Jules. It felt almost completely natural to be around her and share even the

Steve Wilhelm's: Another Time To Love

most intimate of moments, laughter and the casual banter we used to engage in daily.

I could easily see myself settling into this reality and living it out for the long haul. As much as I love Betty and will miss the fact she is not here in this reality, truthfully, Jules was my first love and for whatever reason, it appears now that I have her back. The only thing that's nagging at me, is ever since the beginning of this ordeal, my messing with my past, there must be a price to pay, right? Who knows what the cost of having Jules back will be? I sure don't.

I got up from the kitchen table and rinsed my coffee mug out in the sink and set it in the rack to dry. It was time to go and pay Jeff a visit.

I pulled into the parking lot of the Newcastle Country and Golf Club and at once began to scan for Jeff's black Expedition. It always stood out to me because it was always dirty and never seemed to get the wash it deserved. I loved his license plate frames because they were all Jeff: "I'd rather be golfing." Of course, this was all supposing he even has that vehicle what with all the things I've changed. Or, the job! Then, when I turned the corner into another row of parking stalls, I saw it. However, this Expedition appeared to be just off the showroom floor, brand new. I know it's Jeff's because he'd transferred the plate frames from the original. He must be doing extremely well to have afforded a brand-new SUV, I thought. Good for him!

Steve Wilhelm's: Another Time To Love

After parking my car, I made my way to the Pro Shop from the parking lot. The bell above the door signaled my entrance.

"Be right with you," Jeff's voice came from the stockroom on the left side of the shop. Good to know he's alive.

He came out of the stockroom balancing two heavy looking boxes in his arms, with a pencil tucked away behind his right ear. He certainly was like the golf pro I always remembered seeing him as, wearing casual slacks, a pullover golf shirt and a matching sweater vest. "What can I help you with?" he asked me with a friendly smile. There was no look of recognition on his face, however. This was not a good sign.

"Jeff? You're kidding, right?" I asked, slight apprehension in my voice. "You know who I am, don't you? Please tell me you do."

Jeff set the boxes down on the counter and seized me up and down curiously for a moment before busting out in laughter. "Oh, MAN, the look on your face," he said between guffaws. "I wish I had my phone out so I could have taken a video. It clearly was a YouTube moment."

"I knew what you were doing the whole time," I said, relieved.

"Oh *sure*," Jeff laughed again. "I don't think you could make that expression on purpose, even if you tried!"

Steve Wilhelm's: Another Time To Love

"I've just been a little out of it lately, is all," I explained. "But, hey! That's a really nice new rig you've got."

"Well, thanks," Jeff answered, looking a little surprised. "But, you know how weird that just sounded?"

"What do you mean by that?" I really didn't know.

"Dude, you were right there with me when I got it! You wanted to make sure that everything worked as it should." He reached out and felt my forehead. "I heard that you were really sick there for a week. You sure you're okay now?"

"Yeah, for the most part, I think so." I responded lightly.

"Sorry I haven't hung around with you as much lately, it's just been crazy busy since my new line of golf wear came out."

"Oh, wow, I'm truly impressed, Jeff!" I blurted out.

"So impressed you really don't remember anything about it," Jeff scoffed.

"That's something I wanted to talk with you about," I began. "I seem to be having some issues and I need your wisdom, like you're always so good at sharing with me."

"Well, of course," Jeff said, "but the timing for that couldn't be worse, unfortunately. I just had a huge shipment of clothes come in, but before I can even put them out, I have to do a complete inventory of my shop. Very time consuming, and I have today and tomorrow to get it all done. The sale starts Friday. Can we get together next week? I'll have lots of time to give you."

Steve Wilhelm's: Another Time To Love

"That's fine, really. I did kind of show up unannounced, not much advanced notice, I know."

"Any other time, I'd say screw work and let's go!" he confirmed.

"But, now you're the bigshot pro, shop owner with your own line of apparel! You've hit the big time, brother!" I clasped him on the shoulder. "I'm so damn proud of you!"

"Now, if you hug and kiss me, we'll have some issues," Jeff said, looking around to see if anyone was watching us, then he laughed. "Thanks for saying that, it does mean a lot to me. You're practically the only family I have and you always seem to be there for me."

"We go way back, don't we?"

"Practically to the Stone Age," Jeff snorted. "Give me a shout Sunday evening, and let's make some plans. Meanwhile, get some more rest, get back to being you and get that memory back in order, would you?"

We shook hands and then Jeff hugged me quickly and pushed me away.

"Yup, I know, get back to work!" I smiled and went to the door, hearing the bell signaling my departure.

***

I was mentally exhausted when I finally got home from my first day back at my job. If I had been wondering about consequences stemming from my meddling, I sure found out what one of them was today. It was like I

Steve Wilhelm's: Another Time To Love

walked into a new job where only I knew the bare minimum about what I was supposed to do. I was no longer in charge of software development, a position which I had successfully held for many years. Now, I find out that I am one of the leads in the marketing and sales department, which would be fine in any other circumstance I would assume. The problem for me, is I know virtually nothing about marketing.

I went to the refrigerator and pulled out two cold bottles of beer. Thinking twice, I went ahead and grabbed the whole six-pack. It would save me having to make several trips to re-up my beverages. I always strive for efficiency. By the time Jules got home from her own job, I was already working on the fourth bottle.

She set her purse down on the coffee table and plopped herself on the couch next to me, reaching for a beer. "Glad I made it home in time for one of these before they were all gone," she said, smiling at me.

"Oh, yeah, sorry Hun. I wasn't going to drink them all by myself, I swear."

"Uh huh, sure," Jules answered. She twisted the cap off and took a long swig. "I'd ask you how your day went, but judging from what I see, I would venture to say it didn't go all that well."

"How perceptive," I said as I chugged the last of my bottle and set it awkwardly on the table, narrowly managing to keep it from tipping over on its side. It had been several hours since I had eaten anything and I was feeling the effects of the alcohol.

Steve Wilhelm's: Another Time To Love

"Danny, that was just a little sarcastic, don't you think?" Jules looked a bit put off by my comment. She pushed out her lower lip.

"You're right," I agreed. I took a deep breath and smiled, but I think it was more of a grimace. "It was brutal, to say the least."

"Wanna talk about it?" She put a hand on my arm and squeezed. "I'm always good at listening."

"There's really not much to say, other than I'm totally unqualified for sales and marketing," I said, shaking my head in despair.

"What happened to make you say that? You were essentially over the moon with happiness when they accepted your transfer."

"I was?" I didn't know what she was talking about of course. If I didn't have a major buzz, I would probably think twice before randomly blurting out responses, but it was too late.

"Are you having fun with me? I thought it was your idea to make the change."

"Oh —well . . ." Crap, I thought. More uncertainties were rearing their ugly heads at me. It was starting to get overwhelming. "I guess at the time it may have seemed like a good idea. I mean, learning new things, diversifying, but maybe now not so much…now."

Jules was briefly silent as she considered me, trying to figure everything out. I could tell she knew something was going on that I wasn't telling her. "I'd be lying if I said

Steve Wilhelm's: Another Time To Love

I wasn't a little bit worried about you Daniel," she said, concern written all over her face.

"Oh, come on, I'm fine," I said and looked away.

"No, I mean it. You can't even look at me when you say that. Ever since you woke up from your stupor from being sick, you've been acting very weird, certainly not yourself."

"I'm not sure we need to make a huge deal about this Jules," I said. "I'm just feeling a little stressed right now. Maybe we should consider taking a vacation. Go somewhere, unwind and have some fun."

Jules looked at me curiously, but then it seemed like she was playing out the pros and cons of getting away. Then she focused on me. "I'm not convinced that would really solve anything," she said. "But having said that, I do think it sounds like something we could think about."

The sound of the telephone ringing in the kitchen startled me. I instinctively felt for my cell phone. It was in my pocket. That's the ring of a landline, I thought. When did we get a landline? Jules got up and started walking to the kitchen. "Don't mind me, I'll get it," she said. She came back a moment later. "Honey, it's for you."

"Who is it?" I asked.

"It's your mom."

"My . . . mom?" I tried not to sound as shocked as I felt. I thought she had died from pneumonia years ago! What the hell am I going to find out next? I had to process. I couldn't just pick up and talk to mom like

Steve Wilhelm's: Another Time To Love

everything was fine. How would that go over? 'Hi mom, nice that you didn't die after all,' probably wouldn't be the best opening line to her. "Uh . . . can you tell her I'll call her back? Just say I'm in the shower or something?"

"*Daniel Allen*! What the hell is wrong with you??" Jules exclaimed.

"Look, I've got a headache and a major buzz going on and I don't want to talk to mom like this, okay? Please Jules? For me?"

"In the whole time I've known you, you have never ever asked anything like that. You and your mother are like the best of friends. I've seen you blitzed out of your mind and still chatted away with her."

I looked at Jules and didn't know what else to say. All I could do is sit next to her and look pathetic.

"Fine," Jules huffed defeated. "I'll lie to your mother this time, but I swear, I'm going to set up an appointment with Dr. Stevens as soon as possible. Something is wrong and I'll be damned if I'm going to sit back and let you do nothing about it!"

CHAPTER FOUR

"So how have you been since the last time we met?" Dr. Stevens asked me after shaking my hand with a stead grip. He went behind his desk and sat down complacently as he picked up his pen for notes.

"I'm fine," I stated bluntly. I sat down on the couch to make myself as comfortable as I was going to get. I was tired, and If I wasn't careful, I could very easily find myself nodding off.

"Correct me if I'm wrong," The Dr. began, "but I get the distinct feeling you don't necessarily wish to be here today." He scribbled something down on the yellow notepad clasped to a clipboard on his desk.

He was exactly right, after all. I needed to mellow out and lose my attitude, so I didn't force him to question further. Maybe talking with Dr. Stevens might be a good thing, if I keep my guard up. "I'm sorry, I didn't mean to

Steve Wilhelm's: Another Time To Love

sound so crass. You're right, though. It wasn't really my idea to come and see you. Jules thinks that there's something a little off with me since my brief illness."

"I see," he regarded as the words sunk in. Again, he wrote something down and after he was satisfied with the new addition, he looked at me. "And what do you think?"

"Well, I don't know. I think I'm okay, for the most part. I *have* been dealing with some memory issues though, and that's really been a frustration. For me, just as much as for Jules." It was actually quite relieving me being able to talk about things. I had to be careful not to reveal too much, however.

"Let's talk about your illness. I understand you were in a coma for several days, is that right?" The bottom of his blue colored reading glasses slipped down his nose and he promptly pushed them back into place.

"Yes," I answered. "We're not sure what caused it, but the physician suspects it was probably a combination of fever coupled with extreme stress. I'm not sure, but I'm not a doctor."

"Would you say your memory issues began to occur after the coma, or were you having any problems before?"

"Good question," I said in truth. It was a memory issue that aided the whole ball rolling on my problems. I just couldn't admit to that. "Well, doesn't everyone have memory stuff going on from time to time? Maybe, some more than others . . . but I think I would have to say for me, it's probably been more prevalent since. You think

Steve Wilhelm's: Another Time To Love

maybe the coma is a probable cause?" I would be fine blaming it on something else, rather than my own actions, I thought.

"Well, there *are* things a person can expect as a result of experiencing a coma. There can be states of confusion, speech issues, even post-traumatic amnesia can develop," he paused and then added, "I think the latter is what you may be experiencing." Dr. Stevens sat back in his chair and cradled his fingers.

"That's just dandy," I said. "How long am I going to have to put up with all this?"

The doc cleared his throat and answered, "I have seen, that in cases where the coma has lasted for a week or more, the post-traumatic amnesia can last for months. Sometimes recovery can take years. In your case, being that your coma was only for a few days, your recovery could very well set in sooner. Every individual is different, of course. Things such as gender, race, health issues, that sort of thing can affect the severity and recovery, but as far as you go, like I stated, I think you'll be just fine."

"Is there anything I can do to speed up the recovery? Any treatments or therapy, or anything I can try?"

"I think that time is what will end up being the best thing for you," Dr. Stevens told me. He wrote more in his notepad. "Is there anything else bothering you, Daniel? Any other concerns or issues you have I might be able to assist you with?"

Steve Wilhelm's: Another Time To Love

"Not really," I lied. What was he getting at? "Why do you ask?"

"You're right leg has been bouncing like it has a life of its own for a while now. That's usually a very clear sign of stress and anxiety."

I looked down and saw it was doing exactly as Dr. Stevens had noted. I hadn't even realized it. I must be worse than I thought. "Probably from everything that I've been going through lately, I would imagine." I put my hand on my leg to stop it from moving. It was only through sheer will power I got it to be still. But, I was sure if I took my hand away, it would resume the uncontrollable bouncing.

"Yes, perhaps," Dr. Stevens answered with slight nod of his head.

Did he think I was covering something up? What if I just opened up and told him what was going on. I wouldn't even necessarily have to tell him everything; maybe I could skim over the whole story and abbreviate things. There was the doctor-patient confidentiality thing that he would have to abide by, but if he thought I was totally crazy, could he send me somewhere for my own safety? I couldn't risk that. Maybe I was overthinking things, but I had to watch myself until I was able to get this situation under control.

I glanced at the frame on the wall behind his desk and smiled. "I see you still have Maggie's drawing," I said, feeling proud. It was an astounding realistic rendition of us as a family having a picnic in a meadow.

Steve Wilhelm's: Another Time To Love

Dr. Stevens turned and admired the picture. "Yes, I quite admire it. She was very talented for such a young age, don't you think? How is she doing? Isn't she college age now?"

"Maggie is wonderful. She's a freshman at NYU and absolutely loving it. She came home with Jules to help me, but she'll be returning next week. Jules and I are so very lucky she turned out as she did."

"Please don't take this the wrong way, but I am happy that I've never had to see her again, at least professionally since her treatment all those years ago."

"I must tell you, Dr. Stevens, you were wonderful with her."

"Flattery will get you a lot of things, Daniel, but unfortunately not out of my bill, but I will give you an A for effort." Dr. Stevens said with a chuckle.

We talked for a half hour more and then our time was up. We shook hands once again, and he told me to call him in a few weeks to let him know how I was doing, and if I needed another session, we could schedule at that time.

I sat in the car for a while, with the engine running, watching my right leg bounce. Why was it the right leg, I wondered. The left leg was unaffected, like it was on Prozac. No movement whatsoever. It hardly seemed fair to me. How the hell long was this symptom of stress and anxiety going to last?   I switched the ignition off and pulled out my cell phone. Checking my contacts, I found

Steve Wilhelm's: Another Time To Love

Mom's photo and number. So, the only person who hadn't known Mom was still alive was the current me, apparently. Great. I swiped her photo and watched as the call connected. I turned on the speaker phone function and listened to the ringing. Then, there was a click and I closed my eyes as the sound of her voice trickled from the other end.

"Hello? Daniel?"

She sent chills up and down my spine and I felt a lump forming in my throat. I knew tears were beginning behind my closed eyelids. "Hi mom," I answered as calmly as I could. It was surreal, really, because I so vividly recalled standing at the podium at her memorial service and talking about what a wonderful and loving mother she was. It had taken me quite a while to come to terms with her death.

"Hi Mom," I said, clearly unsure of what to say. There ended up being an awkward silence I couldn't ignore.

"Daniel? You there?"

I shook my head, trying to get out of the funk my brain was trying to establish. "Yes, I'm here, sorry," I replied quickly. "I wanted to apologize for not taking your call yesterday. Jules certainly made it a point to remind me that I've never put you off like that before."

"Oh, Daniel, that's sweet of you to say," she said, her voice sounded cheerful, though there seemed to be some static on the line. "You don't have to be sorry, we all lead busy lives."

Steve Wilhelm's: Another Time To Love

"I understand that, Mom, but I never want to be too busy for you!" I meant that. If there's anything I might be starting to learn from all of this, it might be that you should never take anything for granted in life. Especially, the people you love. The ones that are with you now, or even the ones you thought were gone and find they have returned. "What's going on? How have you been? What are you doing now, can I come over and visit?"

"My goodness, Daniel, slow down, enjoy the scenery. Take a moment and smell the fragrance of the wonderful flowers all around!" I heard laughter in the background, accompanying my mother's own mirth. "The reason I called was I wanted to let you know I was heading over to Leavenworth with some lady friends for the weekend. They are having 'Maifest' this weekend."

"That sounds great, Mom!" I said. "What is a 'Maifest?'"

"Really?" She interjected.

I could hear the surprise in her voice even over the phone. What the hell else have I forgotten about? "Well, just remind me again, please?"

"Maybe I never told you, but last year at this time, we stumbled on it. It's a wonderful German tradition in which they celebrate the arrival of spring by playing music and games, planting flowers and then they raise a 'maipole' in the local square."

"Oh, okay. This 'maipole' is like a flag, or totem pole?" This was sounding kind of cool actually.

Steve Wilhelm's: Another Time To Love

"Well, not just that, but they decorate this pole with flowers, ribbons, cakes and sausages and then dance around it, in the belief and hope that it would bring good luck and wealth to the village during the year. It was a real treat to see last year, so the gals and I decided to do it again!"

"I'm glad you have your girlfriends to be around, Mom. That surely must help in keeping you active and healthy," I added. She used to tell me that an active mind keeps an active body and life.

"Active, of course," Mom said. "Healthy? Hmmm . . . I guess for the most part, except for our beer and whiskey nights. Luckily, we keep those to a minimum of just a few times a week."

"Mom? Are you serious?" I was shocked. "That can't be good for you, I'm sure!"

"I'm just kidding with you, son! Only a few times a month, in actuality. Glad I gotcha, just doing my part to keep you on your toes."

"Jesus, Mom," I said after my heartbeat slowed down just a bit. "You're going to send my anxiety through the roof!"

There was a burst of static coming from the receiver. "What's that Daniel? I think the signal is fading in and out."

"I said . . ." then I laughed. "It's okay Mom, I know there's some weak signal spots between Seattle and Leavenworth. If you can still hear me, let me know when

Steve Wilhelm's: Another Time To Love

you get back, okay? I would really like to enjoy some hot chocolate and donuts with you while we catch up."

"Is everything okay?" Mom sounded concerned. "The last time all of those things were done at the same time, you were out of your mind when Jules and Maggie were in the hospital after the mugging incident in Los Angeles all those years ago."

"Yeah, no, it's not as bad as all that," I said. So some things in this time-line were similar. There was still a mugging, but just not the same outcome.

"Well, listen," I heard mom's voice, though it was fading in and out. "I'll call you when I get back and we'll plan our day, okay?"

"Sounds like a plan," I answered back. "I love you!"

"It was cute of you to call," I heard, and then there was only silence on the line. I closed my phone and when I opened my eyes, I felt a pair of tears run down my cheeks. God! How I've missed you, Mom, I thought. I set the phone down on the seat next to me and put my face in my hands while I rested my head on the steering wheel. I wept tears of happiness, a longing sensation I wasn't sure I'd ever feel again.

During the drive back home, I came to the decision that I would do my absolute best to fit in, to learn everything about this new life I was living and live it to the fullest I could. What could be the harm in that? I had Jules, who I realized now that she was back, I had missed way more than I thought. I even had Maggie still. My good

Steve Wilhelm's: Another Time To Love

friend Jeff was still alive and now I find that Mom is back too! I would do what I could to find out about Betty, but in my heart, I knew that wherever she was, or whatever she was doing, she has always been very resilient. She's most likely doing very well, I decided. I only hope that she is content. I know she would want that of me. I let out a bout of air from my lungs and began to question my life in a nutshell. Am *I* happy right now? Whatever the answer, I will work on it. If it's my destiny to be here, right now, then I owe it to myself to try.

Steve Wilhelm's: Another Time To Love

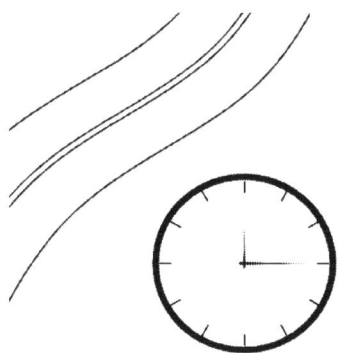

<u>CHAPTER FIVE</u>

This time, as I walked into the house, I felt better and more certain of things than I had in the last few days. My optimism was in full swing. "Jules? I'm home," I said, looking forward to seeing her and playing out the life I never knew I'd have.

"I'm in the kitchen," she answered loudly.

She was standing at the counter with her back to me, and I saw she was cutting up fresh carrots, celery and potatoes. The smell was intoxicating to my stressed sinuses, was she putting together a stew? I smiled and reached my arms around her waist, a warm embrace that I've missed burying myself in.

"Whoa there, macho man," she verbalized when she backed into me, her hands going up in the air. "You realize that's a dangerous move to be doing when I've got a weapon in use?"

Steve Wilhelm's: Another Time To Love

I wasn't sure if she was trying to be funny, or if she was mad at me. There was a different tone in her voice that I couldn't quite put my finger on.

"Sorry," I said and stepped back, putting my arms at my side regretfully. I went and sat down at the kitchen table.

"It's okay," Jules said. "I just didn't want to accidently cut you or myself." She came over and gave me a quick kiss on the cheek. "Where's the stew meat I asked you to bring home? Did you leave it in the car?"

"Oh, crap," I said quickly, rising trepidation filling me to the brim. I actually didn't even remember Jules asking me at all.

"That's just great," she exclaimed, clearly irritated. "One simple little thing I request and you forget."

I sighed. "It's not a big deal, really," I said. "I can run out and get some right now. No worries." I stood up and headed for the back door.

"Yeah, no worries." She changed her tune and moved back towards the counter to toss the knife into the sink.

"Okay then, I'll just go out and get some stew meat and be right back," I said.

"God no," Jules said, turning quickly to look at me. "I wouldn't want you to go out of your way, Daniel. I know you have so much on your mind and all that, so you should just go lay down on the couch and rest. I'll go out and get what we need."

Steve Wilhelm's: Another Time To Love

There was so much sarcasm in her voice I could feel my knee starting to twitch. The tension in the air was physically palpable.

"Jules, why are you getting so pissy about this? I'm sorry, okay? Can we just start over? I had a pretty good day that I wanted to share with you."

"Things are not always about you, Daniel," she tuffed as she got out plastic containers and began to fill them with the vegetables. It looked like she might cry and I wasn't sure what to say, or do to comfort her. I just sat there and watched her put things away.

"Honey, is there something I can do?" My voice was timid, I didn't like it one bit.

Stopping what she was doing, Jules leaned against the smooth surface of the counter. Her face was flushed and she was looking at me, but it didn't seem like she was really seeing me. It was more as if she were just looking through me. "Tell you what, let's just order a pizza. That way there's no reason for either of us to go out, there's no mess to clean up and then we can talk."

"Are you mad at me?" I questioned hesitantly, afraid of the answer I'd get.

"No, I'm not mad," Jules replied, after a beat. "I'm just really frustrated, but I don't know how to really explain it to you."

I wasn't sure I really wanted to know where Jules was going with her thoughts, but I wasn't going to run away from things. I was serious when I decided I wanted to work through things and fit in with this life. "Well, I

Steve Wilhelm's: Another Time To Love

think you can tell me anything. I need to know what's going on, because I feel like I'm kind of in the dark here, and maybe it's my fault."

"See, the fact that you even said that, tells me things are different. You don't remember what was going on before you became sick, do you?"

"No, not really," I said. "I would like to know if you'll tell me."

Jules went to the refrigerator and pulled out two beers, handing one to me. I twisted the cap off the hers and said, "let's go into the living room and discuss this. We can eat later." Handing her beer back, I followed the hall into the living room and opened my own beer on the way to the couch.

I sat down, surprised when Jules sat in one of the easy chairs on the other side of the coffee table. She took a swig from her beer and set it down on a coaster on the table. I took a swallow of my drink and held it in my lap. "Are we in trouble?" I asked gently.

"Daniel, we've been having some issues lately," Jules divulged, looking at the bottle in front of her instead of me. She couldn't even look at me in the face.

"You've got me at a loss," I admitted. "What about the other day in the kitchen when we were kissing and Maggie told us to get a room? You told her how much in love we are and you seemed – we seemed just fine. I'm confused."

"The last four months or so," Jules began, her voice faltering just a bit, like this was hard for her to talk about,

Steve Wilhelm's: Another Time To Love

"It seems as though for whatever reason, we've drifted apart. You've been coming home from work later and later, working on the weekends . . ." She hesitated, as if searching for more words.

"Because of my job change maybe?" I offered.

"Sure, perhaps," she pondered. "But I think it goes beyond that. We haven't made love except maybe once or twice since the holidays, and we used to enjoy each other multiple times a week. We don't talk all that much anymore. It's like the spark that we've had that's burned so bright all these years has lost the fuel that has been feeding it, keeping it alive. It's been feeling like it's burning out and that scares the hell out of me." Her words seemed disheveled, like she'd been running over the idea all day.

Most of me wanted to get up and go comfort her, show her that I do care, that it's all okay, but I could sense she needed the space to keep her thoughts going. I shouldn't interrupt. How could I, or the other me as it were have let this happen to my beautiful Jules? It was starting to break my heart. The old me had no idea what he could lose. "I'm so sorry," I barely whispered. She heard me and briefly smiled at my efforts.

"When Maggie and I tried to get a hold of you for days while we were in New York and you wouldn't answer, of course I thought the worst. I thought maybe you had left me, found someone new, or something." She stopped talking all together. It upset me that I allowed her to even contemplate the idea.

Steve Wilhelm's: Another Time To Love

"Did you say anything to Maggie?" I had to ask.

"No, of course I didn't say anything. She doesn't need to be bothered with that while she's going through everything being away from home for the first time, and her college work load and all. She might suspect something, but I wanted to keep this between you and me."

"Probably a good call," I agreed. "You've always been good with that kind of thinking."

"Anyway, when we got home and you were in the coma, I was so worried and scared that you might not wake up. I would have been devastated if we were not able to have the chance to work together and solve our problems." Jules stopped and caught her breath. She took another swig of her beer and then continued. "When you woke up, all I wanted to do was take care of you, get you back to good health and get us back to being happy. You were different, not quite yourself. It was weird because... not remembering things, it was easier to put aside the distance that had been growing between us." The last bit she said seemed hard for her to say.

"And I guess that explains your reaction to my kiss, when you said I hadn't kissed you like that in a very long time . . ." I stopped as it was making perfect sense.

"Well, honestly, you hadn't. We hadn't, and it was absolutely wonderful! I just rode with it and then Maggie came in and . . . well, I just didn't want that feeling to end."

Steve Wilhelm's: Another Time To Love

"I don't think it has to," I said. For heaven's sake, I just got you back, I thought. You just don't realize that and it's not something I can share with you. I got up off the couch and knelt in front of Jules and took her hands in mine. "Honey, listen. I love you and I never want to lose you, I want you to know that."

She looked at me, her eyes cloudy with impending tears. Her lower lip was trembling. "I love you too, Danny. You are my life, my world, my reason for everything." She squeezed my hands tight as if she'd never let go again.

"If I've been taking you for granted, I'm an idiot and I'm so very sorry. I promise you that I will do my very best, each and every day to show you how much you mean to me. There's absolutely no way I would be the person I am right this very moment without you." I leaned in and kissed her gently on the forehead.

"You really mean that?" Jules asked?

"Of course I do," I said. I tenderly stroked her cheek, wiping the stray tears away that had built up a steady stream.

"Well then, I think you should kiss me like you mean it. Not just some tame little peck on the forehead, you know?" She beamed at me with a bright twinkle in her eyes. She seemed content with our discussion.

"Hey," I exclaimed with mock hurt. "That was one of my best ever forehead pecks. The rest you can have tomorrow." I pretended I was going to get up. Jules grabbed my collar and brought me back down into her arms, as if I'd never left their loving support.

Steve Wilhelm's: Another Time To Love

"I'm not going to let you go until I'm satisfied I've had what I want," she growled playfully. She brought her lips to mine and our kiss was electric. It was better than I can remember, and brought back fond memories of our first kiss on the Ferris wheel the summer after high school. My body felt alive and my nerves were elevated all over, it was a sensation I could never forget. I could only hope and pray that Maggie wasn't going to be home anytime soon.

After breakfast, we got Maggie and her luggage in the car and drove her to the airport. She and Jules sat in the backseat, chattering away, like I wasn't there. I wasn't offended in any way, it was nice to see them carrying on and I truly enjoyed watching them interact with one another. They had a special mother-daughter relationship; they were more like friends. I had a strong bond with Maggie as well, but with Jules, it was just different, special. Listening to them also helped keep my mind in the present, so I didn't think about last night as much.

We watched as Maggie made her way through security and then before she walked towards the boarding areas, she turned and waved with a beaming smile as she readied herself for such a drastic change. The anticipation flowed from her aura, she couldn't wait, both Jules and I could see it. I waved back and Jules blew her a kiss as she always had before parting with her beloved daughter. Maggie did the usual and caught the kiss, rubbing it into her soft cheek. I can't remember when they started doing

Steve Wilhelm's: Another Time To Love

that, but it's the cutest thing to witness, even now. I noticed Jules discreetly attempt to wipe a tear from her eye a pang in my own heart pulled at me.

"It's bittersweet," I ventured. "No matter how old she is, or how many times we've watched her leave, it's still tough."

Jules nodded in agreement and grunted her acknowledgement. As soon as we got back to the car and buckled in, she broke the silence.

"Danny," she started. "I really think we should talk about what happened."

My face flushed with heat and I'm sure ran red. I turned the ignition and revved the engine. Jules reached over and turned the car off and took the keys. "What are you doing?" I asked. "You know the longer we're parked, the more the parking fee is, right?"

"I don't give a crap about any parking fees," Jules said. "Hell, I'll pay them myself, it doesn't matter to me. I'm just saying. I probably wouldn't think twice about last night, you know, but your reaction to it is really what has me wondering if there are more issues?"

"Okay, all right, fine. I didn't want to talk about it last night because I was – still am extremely embarrassed."

"Daniel, trust me, it's not that big a deal. I'm sure it's happened to a million other people, it could happen to anyone."

"Jules, I lost my erection while we were making love! I was fine to start, but then . . . how the hell would

Steve Wilhelm's: Another Time To Love

you think that makes me feel? That's never happened to me before. Ever!"

"Come on, Danny, I don't take any offense to it. I mean, it's not like I wondered if maybe you aren't attracted to me anymore," she commented. "Wait, I do still turn you on, don't I?"

"Of course you do!" I stammered. "Don't make light of this, please."

"I'm not, I promise," Jules answered quickly. I looked intently at her at the risk of coming across overbearing. I hoped for her sake that there were no underlying thoughts of humor or anything in the matter from her. I was already mad at myself and I didn't have any desire to get upset with her any more than I was, what with her pressing me on my bout of impotence.

"I don't know exactly what to tell you," I said, I was tired and the subject was a bit demeaning.

"Maybe when you go see Dr. Stevens again, he can suggest something?"

"Jesus, Jules! I'm not planning on seeing Dr. Stevens again, and even if I was, I'm not going to discuss our sex life with him!" I was starting to get hot under the collar and not all together sure why we were still having this conversation. "Give me back the keys, please. I'm not going to sit here in the car and talk about this any longer. It's just freaking stress causing it, okay? Can we drop this? Please?" I croaked for the hopefully the last time.

"Oh sure, we can drop this. I was trying to be sympathetic and understanding, but if you're just going to

Steve Wilhelm's: Another Time To Love

be a total dick, then here!" Jules almost threw the keys back at me. She crossed her arms over her chest and stared out her window. "Come on, Daniel! What're you waiting for? Let's go home!"

I put the keys in the ignition and started the engine. I slammed the gear into reverse and pulled out of the stall, almost coming into contact with another car looking for a spot. "Fuck!" I shouted, and hit the steering wheel after we lurched to a jolting stop.

This, is exactly what I don't need right now, I thought. I was honestly trying to do everything I could to make the best of where I was, and now little things were starting to creep in and put me to the test. I wasn't faring well at all, and I just hoped I could salvage the damage I may have inflicted on our relationship. Regardless if I meant to, or not.

On the drive home, Jules was determined to stay mad and steadily kept her attention at her window and the slow freeway traffic. It gave me time to wonder about why I failed in bed last night. Was it really just stress? Maybe all this, "mind-travelling" has screwed with my brain and is causing sexual problems. It wasn't as if I ever failed to get a solid erection at even the thought of Jules before, so why now all of the sudden? The more I dwelled on it, the more frustrated I became. Maybe she was right. I needed to talk to someone, but I didn't think it could be Dr. Stevens. It would be Jeff. We'd talked about sex and all that before, we could do it again. I finally pulled into our driveway and before I even got the vehicle into park,

Steve Wilhelm's: Another Time To Love

she had unbuckled and opened the door to get out. The door slammed shut, and I knew it was not an accident. Great, what a night I'm looking forward to, I thought, sadly.

***

Jules brought her lips to mine and our kiss was electric. It was better than any kiss I could ever remember. Blood coursed through every vein in my body, activating every single nerve I possessed. All of my senses became heightened and suddenly my manhood was at full mast. She moved to straddle my body and when she felt my hardness, she gasped and gave me a big smile. "Danny! What is that?" She was toying with me; she knew exactly what it was. "Is it for me?" She reached between our legs and lightly stroked my length through the fabric of my jeans.

"That all depends on how good you intend to treat it," I answered as I breathed hot air on her neck behind her ear. The contact of her fingers made me shiver with excitement.

"Well then," Jules cooed into my ear. Her arms went around my neck and she ground her pelvis into my groin. At some point, she had deftly unbuttoned her shirt, allowing her braless breasts freedom. I couldn't help but gaze upon their magnificent beauty. They were perfectly shaped with no signs of age in the least. I reached out and cupped them into my hands as Jules pushed them forward. She moaned as I lightly pinched her nipples

Steve Wilhelm's: Another Time To Love

between my thumb and forefinger , then I switched to my tongue, alternating between licking and kneading until the tips of her nipples poked out, hard as pebbles, as if reaching for more. First one, then the other I sucked into my mouth and then Jules tensed and reached her hands down the front of my pants.

Her fingers snuck under my shorts and wrapped around the base of my hardness and massaged all the way to the tip, causing me to almost lose it right there. "Shit, Jules," I murmured, breathless. "When did you learn such torture?"

"Mmm, I would venture to call it extreme foreplay," she explained, panting, the look in her glazed eyes I could only describe as pure lust.

"I know what I want to taste," I said as I moved her on the couch so I had better access to the front of her jeans. She pushed my hands aside and unbuttoned them herself.

"Allow me," Jules said, breathing heavily. "Foreplay is officially over. You can taste later because I need you *now*!"

We barely made it to the bedroom and the last of our clothing was gone from our bodies. I put my hands between her legs and parted her folds, wet with anticipation. I was harder than I could ever remember being and Jules stared, mesmerized at it, licking her lips. She took me in her hands and lay down, spreading her legs wide.

Steve Wilhelm's: Another Time To Love

"You need to move your hands, lover, and let me put this deep inside right now, or I might just implode!" Jules was practically begging. I let her guide me where she needed and suddenly I was engulfed completely inside her tight, warm wetness. I could feel her walls squeeze and release all along my shaft. The feeling was incredible. I lost track of time, of everything as I moved in and out of her.

Suddenly I heard Jules voice break through. "Danny? Danny! What's wrong?" I stopped and looked at her.

"What do you mean?" I breathed. "Did you already . . .?" I asked, confused.

"No, but . . . are you . . . you're just been kind of, flopping around . . . for a little bit," Jules voice was small and full of trepidation.

"What are you talking about?" I looked down at myself and saw I had gone completely soft. "How long has it been like that? Did I cum already?" I was almost speechless. I couldn't look Jules in the eyes.

"I don't really know, but I don't think you did. It went down like . . . just a few minutes after we started," Jules said.

"Fuck!" I said

And I woke up. On the couch? Oh, yeah, I thought. I had been banished to the doghouse, but since we didn't have a dog, the living room couch sufficed. Apparently, my brain felt the banishment hadn't been enough

Steve Wilhelm's: Another Time To Love

punishment, so it made me relive probably the single most embarrassing moment in my life. I used to think that mom finding the Wesson oil that I had left out on the fireplace hearth one night after trying something out that I had read in a magazine was the most embarrassing. Now it's the second. Funny how Mom had never mentioned that ever to me, and I hadn't either.

This is the second night in a row that Jules and I have slept apart since I woke up from my fugue. Last night was my own doing, and after I left Jules in bed, pissed and humiliated, I came down here to the couch. She had called after me as I had closed the door, but I pushed her voice out of my mind. I heard her crying on and off through the night, as I barely got any sleep myself. I was too worked up but I think I finally drifted off for a few minutes before Maggie had touched my shoulder and woke me.

"Daddy, why are you down here instead of with Mom?" she had asked innocently.

"Oh, morning, sweetie," I had responded with sleepy eyes. "It's . . . uh, well . . . complicated, Maggie."

"What did you guys fight about?"

"And what makes you go right to the 'fight' theory," I had asked, trying to keep a smile from breaking out.

"Really, Daddy, I'm not twelve! I know these things."

"Well, it was nothing, really, nothing to be concerned about," I had said, getting off the couch. "Are you all packed and ready to go? Or, do you want to stay home with your old mom and pops for another week?"

Steve Wilhelm's: Another Time To Love

"I think I'm good, really, but thanks. It'll be easier for you guys to do your thing on the couch, in the kitchen, or wherever any time of the day or night— when I'm not here," she added.

"Never going to let us forget that, are you?" I had asked, actually laughing out loud.

"No way!" Maggie had burst out in her own laughter, just as Jules appeared with a smile.

"What's with all the noise down here, hard to get any beauty sleep with all of this racket," she had said. Jules didn't need make up to look beautiful. Even with her hair in a tangle from the pillow and bed lines on her face, it was enough to soften my heart and almost make me forget why I was on the couch in the first place.

But, that was the first morning. I had to get through the rest of this night to see what tomorrow morning would bring. Hopefully, without any more dreams.

Thankfully, I slept soundly without another merciless dream. Actually, I couldn't recall any other dreams at all. When I awoke, the sun was shining on my face through the bay windows across from the couch. I stretched and finally glanced at my watch to see how much time I had before I had to leave for work. The digital read out said 10:15 and I literally jumped off the couch and dashed down the hall and up the stairs to the bedroom. I barely caught myself on the landing before I toppled over the runner in the hall.

Steve Wilhelm's: Another Time To Love

"Shit!" I exclaimed loudly. I was supposed to be at work at eight o'clock! Why didn't I remember to set my watch alarm? Better yet, why couldn't Jules have had the decency to wake me up before she left? Was she *that* pissed at me? I had a bad feeling about how this morning was going to go.

Despite the speeding ticket I acquired, I made it to work in decent time, though my fears were answered right as soon as I got to my desk and sat down. My phone buzzed. I picked up the receiver. "Daniel Allen," I answered.

"Good *morning*, Daniel," came my boss's voice. Normally, Larry Tate was a happy, jovial man with a booming, friendly voice, but today wasn't normal. Today his voice wasn't pleasant in the least. "I need to see you in my office, *now*." Then, I heard fumbling and a loud click, as Larry must have replaced the receiver into the cradle pretty hard.

Well, I thought, I might as well get this over with. What's the worst that could happen? I didn't have a job when I got this one. I slowly walked down the corridor to Larry's office, like a man walking down death row to his fate. The door to his office was already ajar, but I knocked lightly anyway. "Ah, Daniel," Larry said as I peered around the door. "Yes, come in and close the door behind you."

I stepped in and glanced on the floor to see if there was plastic wrapping in place to catch the blood from my murder. Further investigation showed me that there was no wrap, just the carpet. I sat in the chair in front of his

Steve Wilhelm's: Another Time To Love

large mahogany desk and waited for the shouting fest to begin. "I'm so sorry, Larry," I said, shaking my head. "I woke up late, got a speeding ticket on the way here and—"

Larry put a hand up to stop me from going on. "I try to be fair to all my associates," he stated coolly, his voice was now subdued. "Do you think I'm a fair person? Do I treat you right? With respect?"

"Well sure, of course you do," I agreed, wondering where the hell he was taking this conversation.

"Two things are on the top of my list that I ask of everyone who works for the company. I adhere to them myself, as I won't ask anyone to do anything I would not do myself. The first, is everyone arrives to work on time, even ten minutes early and be ready to roll. Second, is that everyone put their best foot forward, every day. Give one hundred and ten percent to the job."

"I understand that, completely. Absolutely," I added.

"You're a good person, Daniel. I really like you. You *say* you understand, but I'm just not seeing the evidence that you *do*."

"I—" Larry interjected for the second time.

"Let me finish, please," a perturbed expression now formed on his face. "You missed the morning sales meeting, which I assumed you understood was important. You were supposed to present the statistics on the Danson account. Is this ringing a bell?" My arrogant boss raised a tight fist in the air, shaking it in the air to signal the sound of a ringing bell.

Steve Wilhelm's: Another Time To Love

"Fuck," I muttered under my breath and looked away.

"Your team covered for you, but I'm clearly not pleased with you dropping the ball here," Larry stated firmly. He paused, collecting his strategic thoughts and then continued. "Having said that, I do understand you've been sick, so I can guess that you might still be dealing with the aftermath of that. It's natural, but is there anything else going on that you want to tell me that might be affecting your general well-being? Anything I should know about? I might be the boss, sure, but that doesn't mean I don't care about things." Larry's demeanor seemed to change suddenly. His up and down emotions were throwing punches at me that I didn't know how to dodge.

"No, there's not really anything I can tell you," I lied, but, of course, in my mind I continued with 'because if I did, you wouldn't believe me and you'd send for the boys in white to cart me away in the windowless van to the place with padded rooms."

"Well, all right then," he stared at me letting out a drawn sigh, almost like a grandfather would before doling out punishment to his mischievous grandson. "Go home, Daniel." His words were stark, and gave the impression that he'd given up on me.

"Am I fired?" I queried, so scared of the answer I might get that my heart sank to the pit of my stomach.

"No, of course not," Larry answered. "Take the rest of the week off. Rest, recuperate, get away with the wife for the good R and R. Do whatever you need to do to be able

Steve Wilhelm's: Another Time To Love

to come back and excel at your job." He was the worst. Why did he leave me hanging like that? Make me think I'd lost my hard-earned job. A job I had no idea how to even work?

I sat back in the chair, not just a little surprised, but also a little more at ease. "Thank you, sir," I acknowledged gratefully.

"Sir?" Larry laughed lightly. "You don't need to be so formal, Daniel. His voice was not quite as somber now. "This is not a paid vacation, by any means. We have a business to run, and if you aren't working, I can't see paying you. But you're not fired."

"I do understand," I said, standing properly and feeling more relieved than I had in a while.

"Just come back being yourself again, would you? I miss *that* Daniel." Larry stood as well and we shook hands firmly. The meeting wasn't what I expected, but I'd take it. I even got time off! I left the room feeling more lost than ever, but at least I'd been given time to figure out who this, *old Daniel* was. I closed the door behind me and headed down the hall on a mission to figure out who I used to be.

"Truthfully, I miss that Daniel, too," I said to myself. "More than anyone..."

Before I left work, I sent an email to everyone on my time, explaining I was going to be on leave for the rest of the week. I updated them on the current projects and told them I would check emails if there was anything they needed. I thanked them for covering for me during the

Steve Wilhelm's: Another Time To Love

morning meeting and wished them a good week. In truth, they'd saved me and I owed them as much. Shaking off my distasteful morning, I walked out of the building to the car. It felt weird being off work like the light of the day on my face, but even stranger being off without pay. Even if Jules were to decide to talk to me again, I doubted she would have any kind words to say when I tried to explain what happened. What was I even supposed to tell her? 'I'm sorry Hun, I know I failed in the bedroom, but now I've failed at the job.' Yeah, that would go over just dandy, I thought. There was no way I would even face her right now, regardless. But I knew who I *could* face.

    As I parked in front of Mom's house, something odd occurred to me, something I was surprised I hadn't thought about before now. The house Jules and I lived in was not the same as it should be, or as it was. In the other reality, where Mom had died, I had inherited the house. It hadn't dawned on me that our house was not hers. I'm sure that isn't the only thing I've missed. What a mind-boggling mess. If something so drastic could change like that, what else was in store for me?

    I headed up the walkway to the front door. Mom had changed it from the regular paved path at some point. She had put down circular ornamental stone pieces, spaced evenly up the whole way from the sidewalk. They sat on brown and white crushed rock and was visually striking, adding to the charm of the house. She answered the door shortly after I had knocked and reached out to

Steve Wilhelm's: Another Time To Love

hug me. I let her wrap me up in her arms, surprisingly strong for her age, and when she went to release me, I hung on for a few seconds more. "Mom, I can't tell you how good it is to see you again," I said in her ear. I pulled back and she had a quizzical look on her face. "What, Mom? What's wrong?"

"Oh, nothing, really, I don't think." She shook her head and smiled. "It is odd, though. I had a flash of déjà vu just now. It was like you said the exact same thing before to me, but perhaps a long time ago." She looked at me intently. "Should I be worried about you, Daniel? There's something about you that's not quite right I think."

Having Mom worried about me was like being back in childhood days, and resurfaced so many long-forgotten memories. It was all I could do to keep the tears at bay that were threatening to flow. There have always been times in my life that being with Mom when things were bad made me feel safe. I could always count on her to say the right things or wave her hands, wiggle her nose, *something* to make her mom magic happen. This was definitely one of those times. I felt like a little kid again, in a good way. I'd finally gotten what I'd always wanted; to see her again.

"Mom," I began, my voice tiny as it fought its way around the huge lump in my throat that had shown up unannounced. "My life is so out of control right now, I can't even begin to tell you. I I feel so lost, I don't know

Steve Wilhelm's: Another Time To Love

what I'm doing anymore." I'd let almost all of my drama out in one sentence without even so much as a breath.

The look of compassion and love on Mom's face could melt an iceberg in the frozen Arctic Ocean like the sun shining at a million degrees. She opened her arms up again. "Come here, baby," she said and I fell into her embrace. "Let's go into the den and you sit down. I'll go make us some nice tea and you tell me all about it."

How could I say no to that offer? Of course, if she had told me to leave Jules and move back home or build her a castle, I would say when and how high, like 'I'm on it Mom!!' I was very fragile at the moment and I really needed to be careful of exactly what or how much to reveal to her. Mom has always told me how much she loves me and that no matter what I did or said, that her love would always be unconditional, but I feared this particular 'what' might be too much.

Mom came back into the room with the tray she used to bring me food on when I was home sick with the flu. I marveled at how quick she had prepared the offering – two mugs of steaming hot water with tea bags already floating in them, steeping. She also had included a jar of honey, sugar cubes and freshly cut lemons to squeeze, everything needed for a good mug of tea.

"Thanks, Mom," I said as she set the tray on the table in front of the couch and sat down next to me. "You always know how to make things better."

"I haven't really done anything, yet," Mom replied. She laughed good naturedly and stirred the bags around

Steve Wilhelm's: Another Time To Love

in the mugs, letting the tea steep for a few minutes longer. Finally, she picked up her mug and took a sip after blowing on the liquid. I put a sugar cube in and squeezed a drizzle of honey before I was ready to taste my own. Mom set her mug down and looked at me in contemplation. "Are you taking more sick days?" she asked. "I guess that would be a no-brainer being you are here instead of at work."

"Well, that's just the thing," I said, dreading telling on myself. "They could be construed as sick days, but I am not getting paid. My boss actually told me to take the rest of the week off, but without pay. I really screwed up, Mom."

"Why, what did you do?"

"I overslept this morning, was extremely late for work and to top it off, I got a ticket for speeding on the way there."

"Oh, Daniel, I'm so sorry to hear that," Mom said genuinely. "Did the power go out? How late was Julia?"

"No, the power was fine. Jules was fine. The thing is, we . . . uh . . . had a fight and I slept on the couch last night. I didn't even think to set any alarms or anything."

"Oh?" Mom's eyebrows arched sharply. "The *couch*? If you couldn't sleep in your own bed, why on earth would you take the couch and not the bed in your guest bedroom?" The look of disappointment on Mom's face I remembered well from when she used to reprimand me for whatever trouble I used to get into years back. It

Steve Wilhelm's: Another Time To Love

was enough to almost make me start to cry. She was not pleased.

"It's no big deal, really Mom," I explained when I made sure the tears were not going to flow. "I mean, except for . . ." I thought about all the shit I just went through because of the whole situation. "Okay, I see your point. But in my defense, Jules has all of her interior design crap in there, from her classes and stuff, so the room is really not usable for guests, or me. Besides, I'll tell you that couch is more comfortable than that damn guest bed. I don't have any clue how Jules fell in love with that thing. It's so hard!"

"That's really beside the point, Daniel. Tell me what happened at work," Mom asked, though it was more of a demand.

I gave her the abbreviated details of what happened while she listened patiently and respectfully, not saying anything or giving any judgement. Then when I was finished talking, I waited for her response.

"My *word*, Daniel. All that because of an argument? What did you do, leave the toilet seat down?"

"Mom, really!"

"I'm kidding, of course, but seriously, I don't need to know what it was about." Mom hesitated and I wondered if that was a sign that she wanted me to go ahead and tell her anyway.

"It was . . . a personal kind of thing that I'd feel really awkward in trying to explain to you," I said, my face

Steve Wilhelm's: Another Time To Love

turning bright red. I sipped my tea and looked down. "No offense, Mom. I hope you understand."

"Was it a sex thing?" Mom ventured out of the blue.

"Good lord mom! Why would you even go there?" If I could turn even more red, I am sure I did. Did she realize she had hit the nail on the head? I was not going to confirm or deny it.

"Regardless, it's none of my business, but I'm sure I've told you before what your dad and I always preached, about arguments, haven't I?"

"Probably," I said, but wasn't sure.

"Never go to bed mad at each other. You do that, and it stews all night long and sometimes it's worse in the morning when it could be the start of a brand-new day of togetherness." She was right, although, I wasn't sure how I could have fixed the situation I was currently in.

"This was the second night on the couch, actually," I admitted.

"Daniel, you two really should make an effort to work things out. The longer you let it fester, the harder it will get. Before your dad and I figured out what I told you, there was one argument that lasted a week. I can't remember what it was about, but that was the loneliest week of our lives. We vowed to never let that happen again. And it never did. You've been together this long, you can manage it."

"I'm sure eventually we'll work things out, it's just really touchy right now," I divulged.

Steve Wilhelm's: Another Time To Love

"Does Julia know you're here, or anything about what happened at work?"

"No, I haven't said anything to her about the job. She'll be pissed, that…I'm certain of," I replied just thinking about the conversation I'd have later. Not something I was looking forward to by any means.

"Well, you know, Honey, she's going to find out, sooner or later," Mom told me.

"Yeah, I realize that. Better for me to tell her than finding out—" My cell phone rang and vibrate loudly at the same time. The hairs on the back of my neck and arms stood out. I looked at the screen and saw it was Jules. "Oh, crap," I said. I held the phone out so Mom could see who it was. "This is not going to be good."

"You should answer it," she told me gently.

I pressed the answer button. "Hi Sweetie," I said, as cheerful as I could muster. "How are you?"

"I'll tell you how I am," Jules said, her voice sounding extremely angry. "I just called your work so we could talk and I had wanted to tell you how sorry I was about everything, but they said you weren't there and transferred me to your boss. You know what he told me? Of course, you probably do! He said he'd sent you home and asked that I look after you. What the hell, Daniel! Why were you sent home?" Jules' questions were flying at me like a bat out of hell. I was so stunned I almost couldn't answer.

I looked at Mom sheepishly. My face certainly betrayed my ashamed feeling of being grilled by her over

Steve Wilhelm's: Another Time To Love

the phone. Mom nodded and got up and left the den to give me some privacy before I even had to ask. She always was receptive.

"I'll tell you everything when I see you at home, if you didn't mind—"

"I *do* mind," Jules snapped back, interrupting. Then in a slightly softer tone, "Please, tell me now. I'm really worried about you!"

"Okay, okay," I relented. "Look, I overslept, and then missed a meeting I really needed to be at. Not to mention the damn speeding ticket I got. I didn't have an alarm set and no one made sure I was awake."

"Are you actually trying to put the blame on *me* now? It's not *my* responsibility to make sure you are up and awake every morning."

"No, of course not," I replied. Jules was making me feel very small, and I didn't like it. I wasn't necessarily putting the blame on her, and I didn't appreciate the accusation. "Listen, can we please talk about this when I get home?"

"Where are you if you're not home? At the bar? At your mom's place?" Jules sounded arrogant.

"At Mom's," I said. "What's your problem? Why are you all up in arms?"

"I can't believe you, that you would go running home to mommy before even talking to me about this!" Jules almost yelled through the receiver.

"Oh, come *on*, Jules!" I exclaimed. "It's not like we've been talking a lot to each other the past few days,

Steve Wilhelm's: Another Time To Love

and I didn't want to bother you at your work, either." I lied, I was terrified of what she would think of me.

"Fine," Jules stated simply and then I heard a click and silence followed.

I stared at the phone as if somehow, I heard wrong. "Are you *kidding* me?" I said out loud. "Did you seriously just hang up on me?" I was angry and my blood was boiling. I closed my eyes and began to take deep breaths to try and calm myself down. I felt a hand on my shoulder and turned to see Mom.

"She shouldn't treat you like that, Daniel."

"She's just upset, Mom," I said. "And I sure don't seem to be making things any easier for her."

"That doesn't give her the right to act like that, though," Mom answered.

"No, it doesn't, and I should try to not let it get to me as it has."

"Yes, I agree," Mom granted. She picked up the mugs and everything tea related from the coffee table, placed it all on the tray and finally wiped the table clean. "It's not my place to butt in on your life and problems, Daniel, but here's my unsolicited advice for you. Find a way to make peace with Julia. Even if you have to bend over backwards a bit more than you are comfortable with doing. Perhaps then, she will too. Otherwise, this thing, whatever you both are going through, will fester and could end up unrepairable." She cocked an eye at me as she touched my shoulder with the opposite hand she was using to clean the end of the table.

Steve Wilhelm's: Another Time To Love

Mom picked up the loaded tray, and I followed her into the kitchen, helping her clean up and put the dirty things in the dishwasher as we went. "Thanks, Mom, for listening. I can't tell you how much I appreciate you talking things through with me."

"Well, of course. I'm your mom. I *have* to listen," she said and laughed.

I finished wiping down the counter and draped the dishcloth over the edge of the sink to dry. "Mom, do you think I'm a 'momma's boy?'" I asked.

"Oh, for heaven's sake, did Julia say that to you? Because you're here with me right now?" She rolled her eyes. "No, I don't think that at all."

"It's okay, Mom," I said. "I know you have reservations about Jules, but she is who she is."

"You're defending her actions again," Mom noted, shaking her head slightly. "I don't know where you got the idea that I have dislike, or whatever for Julia, because I really do love her to death! Always have. I don't necessarily care for her random opinionated attitudes she goes off on, but she's truly adorable."

Of course, Mom would say different from what she had said on her deathbed in the other reality, I smiled. I should have expected it and not have been so surprised. "Thanks Mom, for listening. I do love you, but you know that!"

"Honey, I love you too. Now go make up with Julia. Life is way too short for grudges to be held, for partners to be cross with each other," Mom said. "And let her

Steve Wilhelm's: Another Time To Love

know you're the farthest thing from a 'momma's boy' than anyone ever could be, and if she has any issues with that, have her come and see me! I'll set her straight!" Mom scowled.

She followed me to her front door and we hugged once more. I turned to bid her goodbye and then made my way out of the house, hearing her close the door behind me. I walked out to the car and just sat there for ten minutes before turning over the ignition. The more I thought about going home, the more I thought about *not* dealing with more drama. I'm not the person who routinely avoids confrontation. In the past, I have been a big fan of jumping right in and embracing problems. Finding solutions and moving on to the next conundrum was a challenge and fun. Not today, I thought. Being that I'm essentially a wayward stranger in a strange land, it puts a new spin on how I react to things. I feel like someone who has just come across the ocean from the country and the life that I knew so well and have landed in, is uncharted territory. I think I know how the people felt when they got off the boat and checked in on Ellis Island back in the day. Is there anything else my brain can think about anymore? I'm so sick and tired of trying to figure things out, from worrying about what else I've caused, to feeling so damn sorry for myself.

No, I'm not going directly home. It's time to unwind for a bit I think. I'm going to go have a few drinks and try to think about nothing, or anything that is unrelated to me and my problems. I fully realize that alcohol will not

Steve Wilhelm's: Another Time To Love

solve anything, but it will definitely do its job of taking me to that place where my mind is numb. And I'll be okay with that for a while. I think I deserve it.

    I pulled in front of the tavern and parked. This was very familiar, I thought. When I opened the door and walked inside, I knew why I had had that thought. It was the same tavern I had gone to back in my other life, after finding that damn card in the yearbook. I had met Mathew here. Would I have the same luck and find him here once again? I highly doubted it.
    I sat at the bar and ordered a beer and a shot of bourbon. I didn't intend to get smashed but I did want to get comfortably happy. After two beers and two shots, I was on my way to achieving that goal.
    I looked around the tavern and saw the pool table. It had been years since I had played. I was never very good at it, but for the most part, I always had been able to hold my own. I remembered the last time was with Jeff and at the end of two games, we each had a win. The third game I had the misfortune of sinking the eight ball on the break. Jeff won a twenty dollar bill off of me and I'm sure that had a lot to do with my never having shot pool since.
    I heard the bell above the entrance door ring, and turned to watch a couple walk in, hand in hand. They were smiling and laughing, appearing to be so in tune with each other. It was refreshing to see. They made it to the

Steve Wilhelm's: Another Time To Love

bar and sat a couple of stools away from me. I smiled and thought about when I had been that happy.

The girl ordered a glass of wine, and her guy ordered a soda. I don't know why, but it just seemed a little odd to order in a tavern, but who was I to judge, I thought.

"Oh, and give that gentleman a refill on whatever he's drinking," I heard him say.

I turned to face him. "Thank you, but you don't have to do that." I said, holding up a few fingers in recognition to her politeness.

"No worries, my friend, none at all. My fiancée and I are celebrating," he announced.

"Nick, are you planning on telling the whole world," the girl mock punched him on the shoulder.

"And why shouldn't I? You want me to get down on one knee and propose to you, again?"

I smiled as I saw the girl blush and grin from ear to ear. "No, the first time was special enough."

"Well, I do appreciate the offer, I don't mind if I do," I said, standing and reached out my hand to offer a handshake. "I'm Daniel, by the way. If you're buying me a round, I figure it's only polite to introduce myself."

Nick took my hand and shook it. His grasp was firm and friendly. "Daniel, nice to meet you. I'm Nick and this beautiful creature is Gwen."

Gwen smiled and shook my hand too. "Nice to meet you, Daniel."

Steve Wilhelm's: Another Time To Love

"So, you both just got engaged, did you? Congratulations," I . "And likewise, it's nice to meet you, Gwen." Nick was definitely lucky, Gwen was beautiful.

"Are you waiting for anyone," Nick asked me.

"No, actually, I'm just unwinding and enjoying some me time," I told him. "It's been a rather stressful and frustrating off week. I just needed to have a couple of drinks before I go home."

"Ah, trouble in paradise?" Gwen inquired.

"Well, yes and no, but I don't want to bore you with my issues." It was actually good to be able to talk to someone I didn't know. Someone that couldn't tell the differences in me since my jump.

"Oh, that's perfectly all right. This is one of those times where if we played who has had the worst week, we'd love to play! Might even have a good chance of winning the pot!" Nick laughed.

"I highly doubt it," I said. I was pretty sure I could trump anyone at this game.

"Okay," Nick shifted his gaze over to Gwen. "You think we could be up to the challenge?" She seemed quite indifferent.

"I'm really not sure I want to rehash what we've just been through, Nick, do you agree?" Gwen's eyes narrowed slightly as she seemed to be lost in thought.

"It's going to be fictionalized in my next book, so I need to keep it fresh," he answered back. "After the first one, I would've agreed not to rehash it so soon, but it

Steve Wilhelm's: Another Time To Love

could be liberating now. However, this time it involves you, so I would respect you if you didn't want me to."

"You're a writer?" I asked, curious on so many levels.

"I'm working at it," Nick replied with a grin.

"Don't listen to him," Gwen interrupted. "He's just being totally modest. Nick has three books out, all awesome and doing very well!" She grinned at Nick with a wonderfully proud look on her face. "He takes things that happen in his life and fictionalizes them a bit and the readers love it!"

Nick sipped on his soda and rolled his eyes at her statement about his writing skills. "She's right, Daniel. Though in truth, I would love for my next book to be something completely made up, and nothing that I had to actually live through." He scoffed a bit and continued slurping down his soda.

Gwen picked up her wine and held it out. "I'll definitely drink to that," she said and took a long swallow as the wine quickly drained from the glass.

"I'll take you at your word," I declared. "I'm not sure I could accurately put into words about my own adventures, but having said that, I'm sure you could write about them and put out a fantasy bestseller." Uh oh, had I said too much already?

I saw Gwen give Nick a hug and whisper in his ear. Then she got off her stool and headed towards the bathroom without saying much. Nick pulled out his wallet and fished out a business card. "Hey, man, I don't mean to

Steve Wilhelm's: Another Time To Love

be rude or anything, but we're going to go get a booth and enjoy some alone time ourselves. Hope you don't mind too much."

I laughed. It felt good to do so. "That's fine. I don't want to be an intrusion on your celebration." I took the card Nick gave me generously and threw him a hefty grin.

Nick got up and grabbed Gwen's purse from the counter. "Not to push any books on you, but if you're interested, give me a shout, I can get you good deals, and even personally autograph them."

"I'll check you out," I said and put his card in my pocket for safe keeping. "Thanks for the drink." I pulled up my drink in the air and tilted it in his direction.

I watched as he picked up their drinks and moved to a booth in the back. Gwen came out of the bathroom and smiled when she didn't see Nick at the bar. I pointed towards the back. "He got you guys a booth. Hey, congratulations again! Maybe we'll meet again sometime," I mused.

Nice couple, I thought, as she walked towards the back, waving at me as she went. Were Jules and I like that once? I'm sure we were, but that seems so long ago now. Who knows what timeline that might have been in. I have no clue as to how things were in the beginning anymore. I shook my head as I attempted to hash things out further. There I go, thinking about myself again. Damnit!!

I stared at the fresh, ice cold beer and shot that sat in front of me on the counter. No more after these, I thought to myself. I'm okay to drive right now, but after

Steve Wilhelm's: Another Time To Love

these, I might just be pushing my limit. I was a rational guy, I could be trusted to keep my head clear enough. Even if I was going through something tremendously stressful. My intentions were noble, but unfortunately, short-lived. By the time I figured I should probably head home, I had had three more rounds. Two purchased by me and the third by Nick and Gwen after I had sent them a round to them from me.

I stumbled to the bathroom and threw up what little I had eaten that day into the toilet, which made my stomach feel a little less like I was standing on a small boat in the middle of the ocean of ten foot swells. It didn't do anything to alleviate my inebriation, though. On my way out of the bathroom, I saw a pack of Marlboro's that someone had obviously unknowingly dropped. It had three cigarettes and a lighter inside. Perfect!

I'm not a habitual cigarette smoker, though if I had to answer honestly, I would admit to having one or two smokes during bouts of alcohol. Drinking isn't something I do on any regular basis, either, especially after I had hit rock bottom after Jules had "died" and Maggie had withdrawn into herself and stopped talking. I'm sure I would had died myself had Maggie not come out of her shell and saved me. I think that since all that had happened in a different time line, my brain figured it was not a problem to do what I was doing now, that I might as well go for it. I've never admitted to being a smart drunk, and drunk I definitely was.

Steve Wilhelm's: Another Time To Love

    By now, the tavern was quite full of lively patrons. Loud music was playing from the jukebox and a dozen or so people were dancing away in between the pool table and the dart boards. I took my chance to sneak out without being stopped by the bartender who would surely take my car keys, or even worse, call the police. Luck was with me and I made it outside without incidence. The cool crisp air filled my lungs, but all it did was cause me to be wide awake drunk. I did my best to walk a straight line, without falling over, but every three or four steps I almost tripped over myself. I would giggle out loud every time. I prayed I would not see myself on social media tomorrow in this state. Finally, I made it to my car and managed to unlock the door without setting off the car alarm. I stumbled into the seat and pulled the door closed, at first catching my coat in the door. I opened it back up, pulled my coattail back in and slammed it shut once more.

    I dropped my keys three times as I was trying to insert it into the ignition and at that point, I knew I wasn't going to be able to drive. I pulled out my cell phone and after a couple of attempts, finally managed to get the contacts list up. My finger hovered over Jules' photo and then I shook my head and turned the phone off. No way in Hell was I going to call her to come and pick me up. I would never hear the end of her diatribe. It wouldn't matter anyway, I figured, because any way I got home, she would lay into me the moment she saw me and the condition I was in. But I refused to call her. I would sooner walk home.

Steve Wilhelm's: Another Time To Love

I opened the driver's door and almost fell to the ground. After locking the car, I buttoned my jacket and pulled my collar up over my neck and started the walk of shame.

It was well past ten o'clock by the time I got home. Much of my intoxication had dissipated by that time, but I was tired and red eyed and messed up when I finally got the front door open.

Jules came running down the hall with the house phone in her hand. "My god, Daniel, I was worried sick!!" she was frantic and agitated, her words almost running together. "I was just about to dial nine eleven when I heard the door. Where the hell have you been?" She reached out and hugged me and then quickly pushed me away. It was no secret, she could smell me a mile away. "You're drunk!" She huffed.

"No, I'm not," I slurred absentmindedly. "Well, how would you classify 'drunk' because maybe I'm tipsy, but I am certainly not *drunk*." Hearing the words in my head sounded funny, and I did my best not to laugh, but finally a chuckle escaped from my lips. Jules did not find it funny in the least.

"Did you drive?" she demanded to know. "Why didn't you answer your phone? I called a dozen times and left the same amount of messages. Are you insane? Talk to me Daniel!! Don't just stand there with that shit eating grin on your face that I so very much want to slap off you!"

Steve Wilhelm's: Another Time To Love

"My darling, my love, please," I mumbled more than said. "Please, one question at a time." I thought for a few seconds. My mind was clearly drawing a blank. "Okay, let's start the interrogation over – oh wait, no, I didn't drive. I walked." I'm not sure why I decided to lie to her in the first place.

"Jesus, Daniel, from the looks of you it appears you had a few falls during this 'walk' wouldn't you say?"

I made a gallant attempt to brush off my jacket with my hand, but only ended up knocking over the vase that was on the table next to the door. It shattered loudly, pieces scattering in every direction. "Oh, fuck," I said in a small voice. "Let me go get the broom and dustpan. It wasn't an expensive piece, was it?"

"Not that it matters, you think?" Jules said. She looked at me with less than pity in her eyes and shook her head. "I don't know what's worse, Daniel, your distance, or this," she uttered, waving her hands at me in frustration. "I don't know what *this* is, and don't really know who you are anymore. If you were to ask me right now, I don't honestly know if I care." The look of disgust on her face was palpable. She turned abruptly and began walking to the stairs. It was clear she didn't want to be near me any longer.

"Honey," I managed to call out after her. "I'm really sorry, I didn't mean for this to happen."

She stopped on the first step and turned her head toward me. "I love you, Daniel," she said. "But that

Steve Wilhelm's: Another Time To Love

doesn't change whatever it is you seem to be becoming. I don't like it one bit."

"Are we not sleeping together tonight?"

"What do you think?"

I watched her go the rest of the way up the stairs without looking back and me, and then heard the bedroom door open and close a little heavier than usual. I could swear I heard the click of the lock. It was suddenly very cold in the house, but as soon as I laid down on the couch, I didn't care. I fell asleep or passed out, I wasn't really sure which, nor did I really care. At that point, I let the remaining alcohol in my system run its course.

Consciousness crept its way into my fogged brain. I fought it with every ounce of strength I had, but it was a losing battle. Then, a moment of clarity presented itself. A last glimmer of hope hit me. What if I opened my eyes and I was back? What if I was in our bed and I went downstairs and found Lizzie in the kitchen, making one of her wonderful breakfasts, wearing the hot sweatpants with the rip in the left rear side. Oh, how I used to poke her butt through the tear, giving her a start and a tickle. She would always say how much she hated that, but I knew better. She loved it every time.

I thought I might have to pry my eyes open due to the crusted sleep residue acting like super glue, but then one lid opened slightly. Ugh. Couch, no blanket. I was wearing the same clothes I came home in last night. I doubt anything had changed at all, I thought disappointed. I had

Steve Wilhelm's: Another Time To Love

intended on doing my best to adapt to where I was and make the best of this reality, but every day it becomes increasingly more difficult. Now, my head was screaming bloody murder and I had to do something or else it might explode. At least, it felt that way. I really didn't think that would add too much to the ambiance of the living room. It would give Jules a lot of extra unnecessary cleaning work that she, I'm sure, wouldn't have time for.

I went upstairs and took a long hot shower, letting the heat work its magic on my sore muscles and allowed it to rejuvenate my spirits. Jules had already left for work, of course no surprise there. I missed her, which almost felt odd, in one sense. Just a short few moments ago, I had thought the same thing about Lizzie. Maybe it was okay to feel like that. After all, I had lived and loved both of them in my own convoluted lives. I was allowed that, right? I'd lived more life than most, and not many could say they had done the same. Was there anyone else like me out there?

After I had dressed and taken some much-needed ibuprofen for my raging headache, I went back downstairs to make some coffee. To my surprise, there was a fresh pot already waiting for me. Maybe Jules had calmed down and was in a better place about things, about us. I saw an envelope leaning against the coffee mug with my name written on the front. Oh, good, I thought. A makeup letter perhaps! I smiled and after doctoring up my coffee with cream and sugar, I sat down and carefully opened the envelope and pulled out the note.

Steve Wilhelm's: Another Time To Love

"*My Darling Danny,*" it began, her handwriting was clear and unrushed, leading me to believe it was a good sign.

"*I miss you so much! I don't know where you've gone to, but you left me with someone who looks just like you, but isn't you. I love you to pieces, ever since that day in chemistry class when you almost set me on fire. I don't ever want to lose you, but I think we need some time apart. You need time for reflection and find some way to rediscover yourself. Reach for that part of us that we once had! It breaks my heart to write this to you, but I feared if I tried to tell you all of this in person, I would not be able to, and you would try to talk me out of this. I can't do that. I want— no I need you to come back to me Danny! Please, respect me and my wishes. Go stay with your mom, or Jeff. Give yourself a week and then we'll talk. Don't look at this as a bad thing. I think it'll truly do us some good. Remember I love you and always will.*

Your Jules."

I blinked a few times and saw a tear land on her name and soak in the paper like a drop of ink dripping in to a glass of water. I stared at the blot for a few more minutes as everything became an obscured blur. There was an emptiness that had enveloped my insides and the pit of my stomach churned with unease. More tears fell and I let them fall freely. I carefully folded the letter up and placed

Steve Wilhelm's: Another Time To Love

it back inside the envelope. I put my head down on the table and wept, letting my emotions take over. I can't recall the last time I had cried like this. It didn't matter though. Had it really come down to this? Had I really screwed things up so royally that my wife was asking me to leave? How much of a screw up do you have to be to fail at two lives?

I couldn't be angry with her, not really. It wasn't Jules' fault. Nothing about this situation was her doing. The blame was all mine. I was the sole owner and it was my shame to bear. My god, I took her away from wherever she was and the life that she had after she disappeared and brought her back. Because of me, she senselessly suffered and perished in front of her daughter at the hands of those damned muggers that day in downtown Los Angeles. My fault. To top it all off, and certainly all my doing, she was brought back once again. Only to have to endure more heartache. I got up from the table and rushed to the kitchen sink to throw up whatever it was that was left in my stomach. It was more of a horrendous dry heave, since I hadn't put much of anything in there since the last time I heaved in the tavern bathroom. I didn't feel one bit better. I washed my face with the liquid soap in the fancy dispenser I don't remember we had before. Interesting I notice that now. I sat back down wearily and sipped my coffee, helping to take the bitter taste out of my mouth.

Back upstairs, I packed some clothes and essentials I would need into a small suitcase. I know she had said a

Steve Wilhelm's: Another Time To Love

week, so that's what I prepared for. Suddenly an uninvited pessimistic thought began to wave a bright red flag in my head. I did my best to push it back to wherever it came from and lock it away, but it was too quick. If you leave, nothing will ever be the same, was the thought. I had to laugh at that. Nothing has been the same for a long time now. What difference would it make? I just wanted things to go back to normal, and doing what she's asked is the best way to do so.

***

I drove to Gas Works Park, in downtown Seattle right on beautiful Lake Union. I needed to think, but also to kill some time. I figured my best plan of action was to stay with Jeff. I had thought about Mom, but I didn't think that was the best idea, no disrespect to her. I knew she would let me stay in a heartbeat, but she would tend to mother me with concern and want to do the mom thing to make things better. I just didn't need that. Jeff would be similar, but Jeff would be easier to manage than my mother. Besides, I hadn't had the chance to catch up with him and talk about the things I wanted to share with him. It was thinking outside the box, but I was confident Jeff wouldn't turn me away. He was my friend after all.

I felt the ease of relaxation as I sat by myself on the park bench. I happily grinned at the two children playing Frisbee nearby. They really could use some lessons, I gathered as I observed each child's throw was way off the

Steve Wilhelm's: Another Time To Love

mark. Another young man was attempting to fly a kite, but was having the most difficult time getting it in the air. Did he not realize there wasn't enough of a breeze to lift it? I had to give him and "A" for effort. I was reminded of the last time I sat in the park. It was years ago, right before I had gone to see Mathew for the first procedure. If only I could go back and set things back, somehow stop that from happening. I shook my head. That's what got me into this godawful mess in the first place.

My cell phone chirped and as I reached for it, my heart skipped a beat. Hopefully it was Jules wanting to tell me she's reconsidered and didn't want me to leave after all. I could only hope. I looked at the call screen and saw Maggie's picture and name. Well, what a coincidence. Was this going to be a social call or had she spoken to Jules already? No time like the present to find out. With a bit of hesitation, I pressed the connect button. "Hi, Sweetie," I answered as nonchalantly as I could.

"Daddy? You okay?" I could hear the concern in her voice. I wasn't sure if either of us was ready for this conversation.

"Never better," I lied, as the silence grew on both ends of the connection.

"What's going on?" Maggie finally continued. "Mom said you guys were taking a break or something? Time off? From each other?" She almost sounded annoyed rather than upset. I'm sure she had no idea what could have caused such a negative thing to happen. We always seemed happy.

Steve Wilhelm's: Another Time To Love

"Listen, it's okay Mags," I said, trying to sound reassuring. "We're just, you know, kinda dealing with some issues. It's no big deal, really." Yeah, right, I thought. Like she's going to believe one word of that.

"*No big deal*?" Maggie almost shouted the words. "Are you freaking *kidding* me?? No big deal, would be like one of you sleeping in the guest bedroom, not leaving the house completely." I heard a sniff, and she paused once again. I waited for her to continue, not quite knowing what to say. "Daddy, are you and mom divorcing?" Maggie's voice was so small I could barely make it out.

If a heart could physically break, I would have felt mine split down the middle at her words. This is what I've done. My daughter is scared and I wanted so much to reach out and hug her, reassure her everything is fine. Parents are supposed to be there and set examples for their children. What example am I showing Maggie? Failure? "No, sweetie," I managed. I hoped she couldn't hear how my voice was cracking, because it took all I had to keep it from seeping out. "Mom and I are going to be fine."

"You . . . promise?" She managed to let out.

"Of course, I promise." I answered.

"Pinky swear?" I could imagine Maggie's big eyes watching my face at that, as she could always tell by my eyes if I was telling the truth. I'm glad she wasn't able to see them now, but I smiled. We hadn't done the 'pinky swear' since she was so young. It was a gentle reminder that my love for her would never change.

Steve Wilhelm's: Another Time To Love

"I pinky swear," I mustered up the words to say through the lump in my throat.

"Good, you better," Maggie replied. "Daddy?"

"Yes, Honey?"

There was a long silence and I wondered if she was still on the line. "Are *you* okay?" she finally asked. "Do you need to talk to me about anything?"

"It's—complicated, Mags," I said after a moment. "Even Mom doesn't know things, not that I have a clue how I would begin to explain." Shit, I may have said too much.

"Are you having an affair?" Maggie's question was simple and straightforward, but it had a huge impact on the way the rest of this conversation was going to go.

"Of course not," I said quickly. That's what I get for talking without thinking. "Listen Sweetie, let's just agree, between you and me, that I may be simply going through a mid-life crisis – and before you say anything, I am *not* too old to be having one." I had hoped she would laugh, but she didn't.

"You sure?" The concern in her voice was heartbreaking.

"I'm sure. You know, I'm supposed to be the one taking care of you, not the other way around," I stated, doing my best to change the subject. "We didn't get enough time to talk when you were just home. How're *you* doing?"

"I'm okay," she hesitated. "I just—," there were shouts of laughter and glee in the background. "Hey,

Steve Wilhelm's: Another Time To Love

Daddy, I have to go right now, but I'm coming back home in a week for a little while."

"What? Why? There's a couple more months of semester left, isn't there?" Something was definitely going wrong.

"I'm still worried about you, and there's something I really need to take care of there."

"You don't have to worry about me," I said, curious as to what she needed to tend to.

"Gotta go, Daddy, love you!" Maggie said, hanging up with the sound of her friends echoing in the background. With the click of the receiver, she hung up and I was left dumbfounded.

What was that all about, I thought? Now I was concerned about *her*. I wondered if Jules would know anything about what Maggie was talking about, not that I could ask her at the present. It would not be a good time for Maggie to come home, though. Too much was happening, and to be fair…at the same time, not enough. Should I give Jules a quick text? I decided against it, in case Maggie didn't want her mom to know. No sense in me causing any additional problems, if I could avoid it.

My phone rang once more, and I saw it was Jeff. "Hey brother, what's up?" I asked when the call connected.

"I'm leaving work now and wanted to know if it was a good day for us to catch up? Wanna come over?"

"You know," I said beaming, "You couldn't have picked a better time to call."

Steve Wilhelm's: Another Time To Love

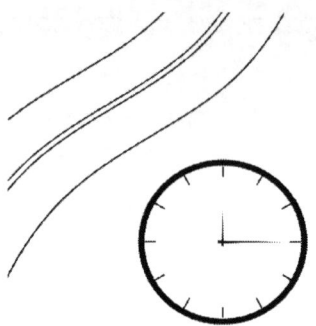

CHAPTER SIX

"That's really messed up, Daniel," Jeff scoffed after I had told him about the most recent events of the last few days.

"I know, right?" I agreed. "I can't believe Jules had *me* leave, either."

"No, I mean that you let things go this far," Jeff rebutted.

"Sure, I see. For a moment there, I thought you might be on Team Daniel," I joked.

"There's no teams. There's no sides here, Daniel. This is family I'm talking about and if anyone should know the importance of family, it should be you!" Jeff went to the refrigerator and pulled out two frosted bottles of beer. "Here, bud," he handed me a cold one and I sat back. "I'm telling you, right now a hair of the dog is what you need. You have to get right back on that horse and tackle that lingering hangover by the tail! Give me that warm beer

Steve Wilhelm's: Another Time To Love

you haven't touched and do the right thing with this perfectly good cold one!" As the spoke, I was happy to hear some of the old Jeff coming out, the one I remembered well.

I took the offered bottle, but honestly, the mere thought of more alcohol made my stomach churn. I didn't even think I could get by with a sip or two at a time. I set it down on the coffee table and pushed it away. "I'm sorry, man, I just can't. I don't want to throw up any more."

"I guess you really went all out and tied on a doozer, didn't you? Was there any booze left at the tavern before you were done?" Jeff laughed, but I didn't. "I'm kidding, you know that. Hey, I understand. I've been there. I know how you're feeling. I'll put both of these back in the fridge for the time being, just in case you reconsider." Jeff did, and then came back and sat down in the easy chair across from the couch.

"So . . . " I offered, wondering how to start the conversation that I really wanted to start.

"I want you to be open with me now, Daniel," Jeff took over, sounding just like my therapist. "You've told me what's been going on, but you haven't told me what's *really* going on."

"Yeah, I know, and I want to . . . but I really don't know how," I said. It was the truth.

"Just open your mouth and start talking. This is me, your best friend. I won't judge your grammar, or your poor use of prepositions, or anything like that. I'm not Sister Margaret Mary from that one year in junior high

Steve Wilhelm's: Another Time To Love

school English class. The one who made us dissect sentences for fun. Just tell me, I'm sure it's nothing I haven't heard before.

I leaned back into the inviting couch padding and linked my fingers together. "Interesting you should say that. Not about the English class, but about having heard this before. You trust me, right?" Here I go.

"Kind of a dumb question, but of course I do," Jeff said. "You remember you even saved my life once, and if that doesn't put you in the trust zone, I don't know what would!" Hearing him say that put me at ease, but I'm not sure he would understand this. It was much more surreal than he could imagine.

Did he mean saving him from the cancer, or was there another time I had forgotten about. I couldn't be sure of my own past anymore. I let that thought go for the time being. "I guess what I want to say is, there have been some changes that I've been seeing lately, things that I know were different before . . . um —" I stopped, trying to find words to describe what had started it all.

"Before?" He asked.

"Look, brother, I'm doing my best here." I felt the beginning of sweat on my forehead and looked down to gather myself. It could be from my body coping with alcohol still, or because it was hot in Jeff's house. Either way, if I had to guess, I'd say both.

"Before..." Jeff repeated, pushing me to finish as he narrowed his eyes as if he was suddenly put the pieces of the puzzle together. Then, his ogles opened up wide like

Steve Wilhelm's: Another Time To Love

he'd just found out the answer he'd written down for the final Jeopardy category, was correct.

"What is it, you look like you won the lottery," I said.

"So these changes you are referring to, we have talked about this subject before, haven't we?" He smacked his lips as he took another draught from his chilled beer.

"Yes, in a manner of speaking, we have, a long time ago."

"I actually thought so. It's making sense now. Weird sense, but it's there and I am going to guess it has something to do with, or began around the time of you being sick. In your coma, am I correct?"

"You know what's going on," I said, though it was almost more of a question.

"I think I may. It's happening again, isn't it?"

"All I can tell you is that I think everything that I thought was supposed to be before I woke up from being sick has changed. Nothing is the same."

"It's weird," Jeff said, "because all that was so long ago, and I'd honestly forgotten all about it. But, then it's like . . . well like Luke Skywalker once said: 'there's a disturbance in the Force,' and it was something I kind of felt. Pretty much the same time as you being sick is when I felt it. When you were in the coma."

"Why didn't you say anything to me before when I came to see you the other day?"

"I couldn't. For one, I've been so damn busy at work, well you saw when you were there. And two, I couldn't be

Steve Wilhelm's: Another Time To Love

absolutely sure you knew and would believe me." There it was...he did know what I was going through.

"I'm so glad to finally be able to talk with you about this. I swear Jeff, I don't know what's real or what my mind has made up anymore. I was so certain my life was finally back to some normalcy and then, BAM! I wake up and find out I've been sick and in a coma? Everything has changed." I ran a hand through my dirty hair and realized just how much I needed this talk with my good old friend.

Jeff had been taking regular sips on his beer while listening to my rambling and realized that it was now empty. He shrugged and set the bottle down. "Tell me, Daniel, what exactly are all these changes you've seen so far." He snuggled back into his chair and waited for a response.

"The first major one that jumped out at me was Jules." I said.

"Your wife? What about her?"

"The Jules I knew previously was dead." Jeff looked at me in surprise. He wasn't quite getting it. "You remember when I was still in Los Angeles, finishing up school and Jules and Maggie moved down there to be with me?"

"Sure I do. Keep going," Jeff said.

"Okay, so there was the day of the mugging, when they were out shopping and never came home."

"I remember," Jeff nodded.

"Well, what happened in my reality, was that Jules died in in that attack, right in front of Maggie."

Steve Wilhelm's: Another Time To Love

"Holy shit," Jeff exclaimed. "What happened that I can tell you, is that Jules kicked ass and fought back. When all was said and done, one of the attackers was dead and the other was seriously injured and spent two months in the hospital before being sent to jail." I had to hand it to her, she could hold her own.

"Jeff, you just called her Jules and not Julie," I almost laughed.

"Damn straight," he nodded. "From that day forward, I had a totally new found respect for her. She's bad ass."

"Huh." I shook my head in disbelief.

"Yup. The whole ordeal made national news, but she took it like a pro. Didn't want anything big made out of it. I think that was more to protect Maggie than anything else."

"That does sound like her," I agreed.

"I guess I can appreciate your surprise, waking up and seeing Jules again, alive. Kind of like that first day that Mathew sent you back and you saw her after years and years of not knowing whatever happened to her."

I stared at Jeff, my mind taking in what he was saying, but it was like it was fighting the comprehension. "What have I done?"

He paused for a moment, really thinking about what he'd say before he opened his mouth. "I think you've somehow created some kind of a time paradox, but potentially on a level that is way off the charts. God, I sound like Mr. Spock, don't I? Anyway, and I hate to ask,

Steve Wilhelm's: Another Time To Love

but you haven't told me about all the other changes, have you. Is there anyone else?"

"Yes," I said. "Mom."

"Your mom? I'm not going to like this, am I?" Jeff wondered.

"She died of pneumonia back before Jules even reappeared."

"The way I remember it, was that she got sick, but eventually got better. So, we put a party together to celebrate her recovery and that's when Jules showed up."

"See how crazy things are? Some things are similar, but still in the end, things are so screwed up." He said.

"So, you ended up with Betty after your Jules died," Jeff concluded.

"And from what you know, I never was without Jules."

Jeff thought for a moment. "Man, you threw a huge boulder into the lake and not only did you create ripples in time, but those ripples created more ripples."

I closed my eyes and shook my head. "This is just a total cluster," I said. "I have no clue as to what to do anymore, Jeff. There's no fix, is there?" He was silent as ever. "Jeff? You are usually my answer man, tell me what to do!" I was imploring him.

"Remember when way back you first told me about what you did and where you were from and you finally convinced me you were on the level? What did I tell you?"

"I believe your words were something like 'Daniel, you're one selfish son of a bitch!'

Steve Wilhelm's: Another Time To Love

"Yeah, that sounds about right and it still holds true. This is what your selfishness has come to now!" He didn't hesitate in the least telling me all this. I had to hand it to him, his honesty was brutal, but it was the truth.

I got up, pacing the living room from end to end. I couldn't sit still anymore. Too much information was floating around my taxed brain. "I need to set things right. I need to somehow put things back to the way they were before. But, at what cost? All the people that would be affected by that ultimate change?"

"What are you talking about?" Jeff asked, though I think he knew.

"Mom would be dead again. Jules would be . . . well, who knows where, and Maggie wouldn't be here because I never would have fathered her! And she's so beautiful and doing so well in school!" I had to stop. I couldn't bear to lose Maggie.

" I would be dead, too," Jeff said simply.

"I didn't want to say that," I murmured back. "I don't want to think about it. Look at what you've done, how successful you are now! You would lose all that!"

"Daniel, stop! Before you changed anything, I never had all this. I was dead. These, and everything you've just mentioned were already a fact, once. It's not like you would be killing, or causing things by resetting the field as it were."

"So what do we do? What do I do?" I felt so damn helpless.

Steve Wilhelm's: Another Time To Love

"Well, I know what I should do," Jeff stood up. "And that is to drink something that has a little more of an impact than beer."

"Yeah, I think I'm ready for that now myself," I said, and we went into the kitchen to take care of things.

I decided to make the first drink a shot of whiskey, just to kind of kick start the process. It almost was a failed attempt, as I tried to thwart the swallow twice, but I was just as determined to be successful. It stayed down. The second shot, fared much better and then the buzz, the wonderful pre-fog came over and said hello.

After deliberation, we concluded that sitting at the kitchen table was the better idea, as it would provide excellent and quick access to refills of our drinks at the drop of a hat. Jeff handed me a pad of paper and a pen. I took them and set them in front of me, not really knowing what they were for. I looked at Jeff with raised eyebrows, hoping for an answer.

"I thought it might be good if we started listing some pros and cons of doing nothing, versus trying to get you back to where you first started. What do you think?" Jeff inquired. It made sense, but I did have some comments.

"Haven't we already established our cons?" I asked. "Like the major one's outcome being re-death. Let alone, also taking away things people have accomplished in their new lives. I'd say those are pretty good examples of cons."

Steve Wilhelm's: Another Time To Love

"Re-death? Is that even a word?" Jeff snickered, by that point we were both slurring slightly.

"Seriously? That's all you got out of what I just said?" It was funny though, I had to admit. We then both busted out in laughter in unison. Our mirth lasted for a good while, until I finally took a large swallow of my cocktail and was then able to speak again without losing it. "Okay, here's another con. I hate my job."

"What is your position again?" Jeff asked. I'm surprised he didn't know. We just talked about it a short time ago. Must be the alcohol, I thought. Maybe we hadn't talked about it? Did I not remember?

"Sales and Marketing Coordinator. It totally sucks," I admitted loosely.

"I see, and what did you do before, in your other reality," he wondered. "Have you always been at the same company?"

"Yes," I said, stirring the ice around in my drink. I pulled it out and licked my finger to taste the sweetness of the whisky. "Only, I was head of software development, which is what I used to be doing in this reality before I apparently requested the change. I'm now basically clueless at this new position and my job is currently in jeopardy because of that. I haven't the slightest idea how to do a position I'm supposedly an expert at."

"Okay, that's a good con, I agree," Jeff commented. "Let's see if we can come up with some pros now. I mean, there's got to be at least one, or two, right?" Jeff thought

Steve Wilhelm's: Another Time To Love

for a moment, then snapped his fingers and grinned from ear to ear. "Jules."

"Hmmmm, pro *and* con." I mused.

"You'll have to educate me because I can't think of any cons with her. I think I used to have lots of them, but they were so long ago, all I can remember is that I just loved teasing the shit out of her by calling her 'Julie,' which I know she hated. Same as you hating anyone calling you 'Danny,'" Jeff smiled as his memories came up to greet him.

"Probably the only person I will *ever* tolerate calling me that is, of course, Jules." I closed my eyes for a moment. There had to be something I could say was in the pro column for her. "Okay, I got it. Pro, because Jules didn't die in the mugging in this reality, so Maggie didn't lose her mother. Pro, because I didn't lose my wife after all the time and effort I spent getting her back in the first place. Con, because I never should have tried to get her back in the first place and you can go ahead and add another con, because of the problems we're having now. I'm not sure we can work through them anyway."

"Too funny dude, you were looking for pros and still managed to throw in several extra cons. Nicely done Daniel, nicely done. I'm sure Jules would be so appreciative of your efforts," he teased.

"Bite me," I returned.

"You wish," Jeff responded.

"*YOU* wish," I said with a laugh.

Steve Wilhelm's: Another Time To Love

"Another cocktail?" He asked me again as he got up to fix himself a drink.

"Maybe one more, but we need to figure this thing out,". I wrote the pros and cons down on the pad before I forgot what they were while I waited for Jeff to bring me my refill. "There's one other thing I need to consider."

"What's that? Have you and Jules gotten pregnant again?" Jeff set my fresh drink down in front of me.

"Oh, hell no! I'd have to be able to keep an erection to completion for that to happen," I said, shuddering at the memory.

"That had to have been the worst moment in your life," he said, true sympathy in his voice.

"It's right there in the top five," I agreed.

"Sorry you had that happen to you," Jeff said. He lifted his drink in the air. "Here's to it never ever happening again!"

"I'll drink to that!" I agreed, and we toasted.

"Daniel," Jeff said, "I think your bottom line is, you need to consider doing what you truly think is best for you, not anything else. If you're not happy, then you should do whatever you can do to get you back to the happiness you deserve. You understand what I'm saying?"

"I do," I told him.

"In life, there are always ups and downs, good times and bad. The point, is that you have to live with the lot in life that you're given. It's not like if you don't think the jacket fits you perfectly, or the comforter you have on your bed isn't really the color you thought you wanted.

Steve Wilhelm's: Another Time To Love

You can exchange those things, because they're just material objects in life. But, the life you have lived, and the life you have, is precious and shouldn't be taken for granted. Not one bit."

"Truly a sobering thought," I let on. "I think I'm understanding."

"You, my friend, somehow found a way to step outside and see what the hell can happen on the other side of the fence, as it were. You needed to see if the grass was truly greener and what did you find?"

"I never should have scaled the fence. My life was good, it really was good. I think I should have let things be." I missed Betty. I missed Lizzie as well, but really, weren't they the same person? Either way, she was my wife. She still *is* my life in that wonderful reality I left.

"None of this," Jeff spread his arms wide, "is as good as it seems, and I'll be the first to admit I like how this life has gone for me, but none of this, I think, is truly meant to happen. If you were able to go back and set things right and this reality blinks out, I'm okay. Cause really, it never happened."

"Is this what being God is like?" I shuddered. "I don't know that I'd ever be good enough, or noble enough to be able to carry that responsibility."

"I don't think anyone here on Earth could be either, but that's a topic for another day." Jeff divulged. "What was that other thing you said you needed to consider?"

"Oh, yeah. It may not mean anything, and certainly won't if all this goes away. But, Maggie said she's coming

Steve Wilhelm's: Another Time To Love

home because she needs to take care of something. I don't know what it is, but she wouldn't just up and leave school if it were something trivial." I still had that anxiety welling up in my mind, too.

"She didn't give any indication as to what it was?"

"No, I thought about texting Jules, but . . . you know. Maybe Maggie doesn't want Jules to know. I just don't know at this point, but it has me worried."

Jeff drained his glass and went to the sink. He rinsed it out and leaned against the counter and stared at me. "So what's the plan, Daniel? I will do whatever you need me to do." He was right, he always was a trooper.

I swallowed the last of my drink. It didn't taste as good anymore. For whatever reason, I felt I was sobering up. "I think it's time to try and locate Mathew."

***

That morning, upon waking, I was thankful we hadn't gone booze-crazy the night before, as I didn't feel too bad. I felt only a slight headache, but nowhere near as bad as after the night at the tavern. A couple of cups of coffee later, along with some eggs and bacon, and my head was clear.

Jeff told me he took the rest of the week off using his vacation days. I tried to explain he should not waste them on me, but he told me if everything works out and I somehow get back, it wouldn't matter if he used vacation now, because . . . well, he didn't have to explain any

Steve Wilhelm's: Another Time To Love

further. I understood. I was just happy to have his company. Jeff had brought his laptop in to the house from his car and once connected to the internet, cracked his knuckles and smiled. "Okay, let's figure some things out. Do you happen to remember this Mathew dude's last name? I'll search for him and see if we can get a hit."

I was drawing up a complete blank. Mathew, Mathew, Mathew . . . I knew it was something generic...and then it came to me. "It's Stevens. That's Mathew's last name, Stevens."

"Perfect," Jeff acknowledged. "Is that spelled with a 'v' or 'ph,' do you know?"

"Give me a break, would you?" I exclaimed with a smile. "I was lucky to remember the *name* as it is!"

"Noted," Jeff derided.

I heard his fingers on the keys and watched as he sat back and observed the screen. Figuring it would take some time, I went to the refrigerator and pulled out two bottled waters and after handing one to Jeff, I sat down across the table from him. "Which spelling did you start with?" I asked.

"The 'v,' and it brought up two listings for doctors. One is a gynecologist, and the other is a theoretical psychotherapist. You think we got lucky?" Jeff wondered.

"Perhaps not with the gyno, but let's call the number of the other one." Maybe we had gotten lucky, I thought.

Jeff gave me the number and I dialed it on my cellphone. I put it on speaker and we heard it ring twice, before it was answered. There was a soft click and it went

Steve Wilhelm's: Another Time To Love

to a recorded message. "The number you have dialed is no longer in service. There is no new number. Message 458269D." I hated that recording. I disconnected the call and set the phone on the table. Jeff saw the dejected look on my face and stepped up to save me.

"Hey, it's our first try," he told me. "And... just because the number doesn't work, doesn't mean he's not there. Maybe he's in the process of getting a new phone system."

"Try the 'ph's' and see what you come up with," I suggested.

Jeff tapped away at the keys again and hit enter. "Damn," he said after a moment. No Mathew Stephens' at all in the Puget Sound area. I'm going back to the first page and we're getting the address of the disconnected guy."

***

After a little research, we found it. According to the address, Mathew's office was downtown Kirkland where Central Way intersects with Lake Washington Blvd. It wasn't easy to find parking, but then we lucked out when someone pulled out of a parking spot on the street a block away. Jeff deftly parallel parked and then turned off the ignition.

"I think this is where you need to go solo, Daniel. You don't need any distractions from me."

Steve Wilhelm's: Another Time To Love

"You sure?" I asked Jeff. "Not concerned about safety in numbers?"

"You're going to see a real doctor, not a Dr. Frankenstein," Jeff smirked. "You'll be just fine. Besides, I saw a coffee shop on the street level of the building, so we can meet there after you check things out."

"You buying?" I asked. "I don't have a lot of cash on me."

"I'm sure they take credit or debit," Jeff said.

I opened the car door and got out. Just before closing it, I looked him. "And you have both credit and debit too! Thanks buddy! You really are generous! I'll meet you there!" I closed the door and moved down the sidewalk, laughing to myself. I'm always happy to treat my best friend to a coffee, anytime, I thought.

The Park Place building is an older structure, built mostly of stone and bricks and probably constructed sometime in the seventies. It seems to have held up to time quite well, and I wouldn't be surprised if it didn't end up as a historical landmark. Mathew's office, according to the information we got from the internet, was located on the third floor. As I entered the building, I was pleased to see two elevator doors in the far wall, which meant that stairs and exercise weren't the option of getting to Mathew. Not that I was lazy by any means, but even I had my days.

The elevator was slow and had a musty, old carpet odor, and I thought to myself that the stairs would definitely be the best way to go next time. I'm sure that

Steve Wilhelm's: Another Time To Love

given the choice of being stuck in this elevator and locked in the stairwell, my chances of survival would be better in the latter, if only for the fresher air to breath. Not that I would vote to be stuck in either place at any given time.

The woman manning the reception desk informed me that Dr. Stevens was out of the office attending a seminar in Portland, but she expected him back on Friday. She asked if Dr. Stevens had been expecting me and I politely told her hadn't. I told her I had met him before when she asked, but that it felt like a lifetime ago. She told me I could leave my name and phone number, but I just picked up his business card and told her I would call him on Friday. Looking at the number on the card, I mentioned it was different from what was listed online. She laughed and said she had told Dr. Stevens many times to get that changed, but apparently, he had not gotten it taken care of. She thanked me for the information and then I left, being careful to use the stairs instead.

I met Jeff at the coffee shop, and as soon as I sat down, the barista server brought over a caramel flavored latte for me.

"Thanks, Jeff," I said, surprised at the drink.

"I was watching for you," he said. "And you're welcome. You still like the caramel flavor and haven't changed to, like, Irish Cream or a candy bar flavored fru fru coffee, right?"

"No, still the same, predictable Daniel," I reassured. "Just like my chicken fried steak and eggs that I always

Steve Wilhelm's: Another Time To Love

order at breakfast. Funny how sometimes I can spend over fifteen minutes and end up ordering the same thing."

"I just figure you'll surprise me one morning with an inspiration to try something else," Jeff said. "So how did things go on the third floor? You got here pretty quick, so I'm assuming it wasn't his office?"

"It was his office actually, however, he wasn't there. He's attending some kind of seminar in Oregon, but his receptionist said he'll be back on Friday. So, at least we have "A" Dr. Steven's lined up."

"Well, now we just get to play the wonderful game of wait," Jeff commented.

"Yes, so it seems," I responded. I sipped at my coffee and looked around the busy shop. The lunch crowd was filling up all the tables. I heard the woman at the counter call out, "Joseph, your order is ready," and my ears perked. "Hey, Jeff, did you hear that?" I asked.

"Hear what?"

"The voice that just called the guy's name," I answered. "I know her." I searched the counter area with my eyes, straining to see the face through the crowd milling around the register. Then, it was as if my desire to see caused the mass of people to part, allowing me to gaze at the woman. It was her!

"Who is it, who are you looking at?" Jeff asked. He craned his own neck around to look.

"It's Lizzie," I exclaimed. "I'd know that voice anywhere." I stood up, feeling an overwhelming need to go and talk to her.

Steve Wilhelm's: Another Time To Love

"I wonder why she's working here," Jeff mused. "Last you told me, she was heading up the Seattle division of the interior design firm she works at."

"I don't know," I said. "Maybe she's doing a favor for a friend or something. It can't be her regular job." Could it? Something didn't feel right, I thought.

"What are you waiting for," Jeff urged. "Go talk to her!" I knew what I was waiting for, I wasn't in a relationship with this woman anymore and Jules wouldn't approve. Still, I pressed on.

I went to the back of the line and waited patiently as I slowly inched my way to the counter. Finally it was my turn and I stepped forward.

"And what can I get for you--" Lizzie said and then her eyes opened wide as when she recognized me. "Oh my God, Daniel?" Lizzie came rushing around the counter and pulled me into her arms. I returned the hug and enjoyed the contact. She felt good. Lizzie slowly pulled away and looked around hesitantly before going back behind the counter. "It's been a long time, Daniel," she remarked.

"Yes, it has," I returned. "Almost seems like forever. How you been?" I lowered my voice and leaned closer to her. "You don't really work here, do you? Not that it would be a bad place to be at, or anything like that. But aren't you like the president of some interior design company by now?"

"Oh, boy, Daniel," Lizzie said slowly. "There's a lot of stuff that's happened to me that you have no idea about." An older woman came out of the back and stood next to

Steve Wilhelm's: Another Time To Love

Lizzie. The stern look on the her face made me think of the lunch room worker at my old elementary school, who would glare at all the kids and send them to the office if they did anything out of line.

"Is everything okay here?" she looked at Lizzie and then at me. It was not a kind look.

"Yes Connie, everything's fine," Lizzie said, clearly embarrassed and uncomfortable.

"Good. Let's keep the lines moving," Connie said and went back to her office.

"Daniel, I can't talk here. They like to fire employees for socializing unnecessarily." She quickly wrote something on a napkin and slid it across the counter towards me. She then picked up a plastic cup and filled it with ice water. "Here you go, sir, we do appreciate your business." She then mouthed the words 'call me,' and glanced at the napkin.

I took the water and the napkin and smiled. "Thank you, I'm sure I'll be back," I said and went back to the table with Jeff.

"That didn't look the least bit comfortable," Jeff noted.

"Yeah, you can say that again," I agreed. "She gave me her phone number. I'll give it a call later on, see if we can get together and catch up." I was actually kind of glad I was staying at Jeff's now. I couldn't see any way of getting out and seeing Lizzie if Jules hadn't of banished me from the house. At the very least, it would have been a very awkward situation if I was still at home.

Steve Wilhelm's: Another Time To Love

"What do you think is going on," Jeff asked.

"Honestly, I have no clue, but I suspect she didn't one day wake up and pick this job as a career change, and don't get me wrong, there's nothing wrong with working as a barista. I know Lizzie, and I just don't see her doing it."

Jeff finished his coffee and looked at the time on his phone. "You mind if we go? I want to get some things for a barbecue dinner and get home to check emails."

"No, that's fine," I said. I grabbed both his empty cup and mine, tossing them into the garbage by the door. Jeff handed me the water and before we exited, I turned and caught Lizzie's attention. I waved to her, flashing her a bright smile. She briefly waved in return and we left. Not much to it, but it lifted my spirits.

Later that afternoon, while Jeff was preparing the burgers for the barbecue, I called the number Lizzie gave me and we made plans to meet for lunch the next day at a café in Kirkland. After my phone call, we sat out on the porch and enjoyed our deliciously hard-earned dinner while watching the sun set. Jeff had cooked up his signature homemade chili, which is wicked good, but I had forgotten about gas and heartburn that always followed. Then, I remembered why I often referred to it as wicked deadly, but those after effects were also half the fun. I laughed when I thought of how many times Jules was tortured by the odors and noises my body produced throughout the evening and night after those meals. I'd never forget it.

Steve Wilhelm's: Another Time To Love

We were just cleaning up and putting our dirty dishes and things in the dishwasher when my cell phone rang. I went to the table to answer it and looked at Jeff when I saw who was calling. "Holy shit," I said. "It's Jules."

"Okay," Jeff acknowledged.

"What do I do?" I asked, immediately knowing what his response was going to be. It was just the first thing out of my mouth.

"I think the prudent thing to do would be to answer politely with a hello," Jeff said. "Give yourself some privacy. I'll just finish up in here."

I nodded and went out into the garage and closed the door. I didn't necessarily care if Jeff heard my conversation, but perhaps, it was better he not be subjected to whatever was going to be on Jules' mind. "Hey," I answered. "How are you?"

"Tell me, what do you know about Maggie leaving school and coming home?"

That's real nice, I thought. Let's go ahead and skip the pleasantries and get jump to the point. No sense wasting any time. "I don't know any more than that," I told her truthfully.

"Why the hell couldn't you have called me to let me know? I could have talked sense into her so she'd do the smart thing and stay there. Shit, Daniel, it's just not a good time for her to be here." Jules sounded obstinate and disgruntled and I was not ready for this conversation.

"Well, frankly, I thought you had other things on your mind," I countered. "And yeah, good luck in trying to talk

Steve Wilhelm's: Another Time To Love

sense into our daughter by the way. You know as well as I do that once she makes up her mind to do something, she won't budge. She's just as stubborn —," I stopped, not wanting to cause any scenes.

"Just as stubborn as me? Is that what you were going to say? I know you want to," Jules ridiculed.

"That's not always a bad quality to have," I said, trying to make what I had almost said better. I suddenly felt a belch rise up from my stomach and as hard as I tried to stop it, it came out quick and loud. "Oops, sorry," I said.

"Are you drinking, again?" Jules asked, her voice was softer and I could almost detect concern behind the words.

"No, I'm not. We just ate some burgers and stuff," I explained.

"Oh, say no more," Jules said. "Jeff's famous chili, I bet. Better you staying there than here." I could swear I heard a suppressed giggle. "To answer your first question though, I'm . . . coping. I think what we're doing is good, you know? You and I taking some time to work through our issues individually."

"Yeah," I said softly. "I'm sure this hasn't been a walk in the park for you though. I know it hasn't for me. You gotta know that I'm truly sorry for bringing us to this." In truth, I knew every word I said was true. I was to blame for all this mess.

"I can't let you take all the blame, Daniel," Jules said.

I heard a click-click noise on the other end. "Are you still there?" I asked, thinking we had gotten disconnected.

Steve Wilhelm's: Another Time To Love

"Hey, I've got another call I need to take. We'll talk more soon, okay?" Jules said, sounding rushed.

"I love you, Jules," I said.

"Be good, Daniel," Jules said and then was gone.

I felt hollow inside. That was the first time I can ever recall Jules not saying 'I love you,' back. Even stressed out, or pissed off at each other. We always managed to say those words before ending calls, or going to sleep. It was just what we did. I shook my head slowly and went back inside.

"Things okay?" Jeff probed. He then noticed the crestfallen appearance on my staggering my face. "Hey, sorry buddy. You really don't have to answer that. Your look says it all."

"Never a dull moment with me around," I half-joked.

Steve Wilhelm's: Another Time To Love

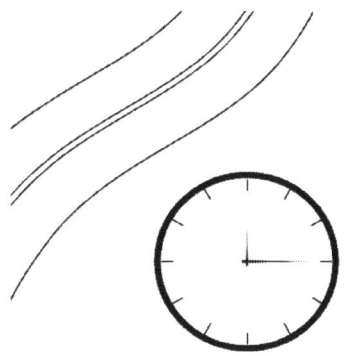

CHAPTER SEVEN

After the hostess seated us in a booth with a window looking out into the trees outside, I got a good look at Lizzie. There was a sadness in her eyes that was hard to miss. Whatever has caused that, I thought, needs to be eradicated from existence. "How are you," I asked.

"I'm good," she responded dejectedly. Her smile didn't reflect what she said and it concerned me, which I could tell she noticed. "Still good at that aren't you? You could see right through that statement, couldn't you?" I nodded. "Okay, honestly? Life has been better."

"I sure can relate to that," I said. "Can I tell you how stunning you look? You haven't aged a day since I met you at the fraternity party at college."

"Also still the charmer," Lizzie laughed, her smile now genuine. "Thank you. You look great as well. How's Jules and Maggie?"

Steve Wilhelm's: Another Time To Love

"Jules? She's . . . Jules. And Maggie? You should see her, she's all grown up now, in her freshman year of college about as far away as you can get from home. NYU. I think she's loving it. She says she misses us terribly, but I'm not sure I believe her," Lizzie laughed at what I'd told her.

The waitress came by to take our orders. Lizzie selected the chicken Caesar salad and I asked to have the chicken tenders and fries. She poured coffee for us and left our table so swiftly we didn't see her leave.

"So Lizzie, tell me what's going on? I know it's been forever, but I do care about you."

"You're sweet, Daniel. I could always talk to you," Lizzie admitted. She took a sip of her coffee and collected herself. "You want the abbreviated or the long winded version?"

"Whatever you feel comfortable with," I said. "I'm not going anywhere." I reached out and took her hands in mine and gave a reassuring squeeze. We held them together for a minute before she let go.

"Things haven't always been like this," Lizzie began. "After you and I split up and went our separate ways, I moved up here to Seattle and started an internship at Reynolds & Davis Interior Design. Shortly after, they hired me full time. I fast-tracked my way up the ladder and was promoted to management and loved every minute of it." Still, even though she had nothing but positive things to say, I knew I was about to hear something negative.

Steve Wilhelm's: Another Time To Love

"I remember you were always very good at that," I commented proudly.

"*Anyway*," Lizzie continued, smiling, "I ended up meeting a guy who had been shopping for a design firm and even though he didn't choose us, we hit it off and started dating. He was a successful attorney and before I knew it, he had swept me off my feet." She smiled sweetly at hearing herself say this.

"That's great," I said. "You know I've always wanted the best for you."

"And it was good . . . for a while. Until, I found out I wasn't the only one he was seeing."

"No," I added, honestly shocked. "Are you serious?" How could anyone cheat on her?

"Yes," Lizzie nodded. "There were at least three or four unsuspecting women he was stringing along besides me. Trust me, I wasn't looking for that, but one day he left his phone at my apartment and I swear, in the course of an hour, he had four calls, all from names in his contact directory. All female names. Of course, I didn't listen to any of the messages they left, but I did ask him about the calls."

"What was his response?"

"Holy shit, you would've thought I was accusing him of espionage. The look on his face was priceless. Then, he stammered and said they were just clients and he couldn't talk about anything. He went so far as to throw out the 'attorney/client confidentiality privileges,' something phony like that. Then, he tried to smooth everything over,

Steve Wilhelm's: Another Time To Love

and got all fake romantic with me and led me to the bedroom and tried to take off my shirt. I could see right through his premise and I pushed him off. He suddenly changed and I saw a totally different side of him divulge. His face filled with rage and he lost sight of his bearings...Daniel, he growled and punched me square in the face, pushing me to the floor." Just thinking about what she'd said made me want to beat his ass for laying a hand on her.

"Oh my God," I exclaimed. "What the hell was he thinking?"

"I somehow got back up and instinctively kicked out and my foot connected right with his nuts. I've never seen someone go down that fast before. I grabbed my phone from my purse. I screamed for him to get out, or I was calling nine one one."

"What did he do? Did he leave, or did you make the call anyway?"

"He got up slowly, holding one hand on his balls and the other out in front. He begged me not to call, that he would leave. I told him we were done and I never wanted to see his fucking face again. It was funny, the look on his face. I got the impression that no one had done this to him before. He limped towards the door and before he left, he turned around and looked at me. His eyes narrowed and he told me, and I won't forget the words, 'oh, you'll see me again, trust me,' and then he left, leaving the door open behind him."

"Did you file charges against him?"

Steve Wilhelm's: Another Time To Love

"No, I figured if he just stayed away from me and moved on, it would all just blow over, but apparently that wasn't in the cards."

"What happened?"

"He had papers served to me at work, charging me with assault in the first degree, which is a class A felony."

"Are you kidding me?" I was seething. "For defending yourself?"

"Yeah, he kind of left that part out. He said he had photos taken of the bruises I caused with my 'attack' along with a doctor's statement that it was probable that he would never be able to produce sperm and be able to have children as a result."

"It would serve him right if that was true," I said.

The food was brought to the table and it gave us the chance to relax a little. Lizzie picked at her salad for a bit before taking a bite. I dipped a piece of my chicken in the ranch dressing they provided along with ketchup and chewed, but I couldn't really taste how good I knew it should be.

"Anyway," Lizzie continued, "I was called into the human resources department and questioned. I, of course, admitted to what I did, even explained the circumstances, but they said that if it went to court, the publicity would cause too much negative publicity for the firm. They said they were sorry, but I put them in a very awkward position. They said they had no choice but to terminate my employment effective immediately. That simple. I had no recourse, but to accept their decision."

Steve Wilhelm's: Another Time To Love

"I'm so very sorry, Lizzie," I said. "When did all this happen?"

"It's been a few years now. I've been bouncing around from job to job, trying to find something that stimulates me, a new career, you know? I've been more or less blacklisted from the design industry, labeled difficult to work with, something crazy like that."

"That's just so fucking unfair," I said. I wanted to break something, pound something into the ground until it was beyond recognition.

"It's just what I've had to deal with, Daniel. I must have done something really bad in a previous life or something, so this is now my destiny."

"I don't believe that, not at all," I told her. "You're a wonderful, awesome person, that deserves nothing but the best. That prick is the one who needs to have Karma pay him a nasty visit."

"You're so sweet, Daniel," Lizzie said. She looked down at her salad and moved the food around the plate absently. "I'm sorry, I can't really eat anymore. It's just not appealing to me like I thought it would."

"Hey, let's get out of here, go for a walk, get some air," I suggested. "I don't think either of us is much interested in our lunch anymore."

"That actually sounds divine," Lizzie said with a grin. She left the table to use the bathroom while I went to settle up on the tab.

Steve Wilhelm's: Another Time To Love

We left Lizzie's car in the café parking lot and I drove us down to the waterfront where I then parked. It was a beautiful, sunny and warm day, perfect for a stroll. She suggested we sit on a bench and just enjoy some quiet time for a bit, which I happily agreed to. We watched a couple of children having a grand time playing fetch with their German Shephard and a very used tennis ball.

After a while, Lizzie finally spoke. "Do you ever wonder about things, what if's and stuff like that?"

"Funny you should say that," I said. "I do wonder about that, actually quite a bit lately."

"How come you do?" Lizzie turned and looked at me. Her hair shimmered in the sunlight. I had forgotten how pretty Lizzie was.

"Well, you know, like don't you ever wonder how if you'd done things differently, how things might have turned out? Like in your case, for instance. If you'd never met that prick who did all that to you, maybe you'd be the CEO, or something else even better at that firm?"

Lizzie reached over and put her hand on my arm. "What's going on with you, Daniel? I'm not sure I remember you being so whimsical, almost melancholy. Are you having those thoughts? Is life not all rosy and wonderful for you?"

I looked at Lizzie and baffled at her questions. "Things are . . . difficult . . . with Jules right now," I said.

"What did you do?"

"Why would you automatically assume it was something I did?" I asked.

Steve Wilhelm's: Another Time To Love

"I wasn't," Lizzie said, smiling. "I was kidding. You obviously didn't see the twinkle in my eyes I guess." Lizzie lightly caressed my arm. "I'm sorry, Daniel. Is it so bad you guys can't work things out?"

"Honestly? I really don't know. My life is so—," how could I tell her anything without actually telling her the truth? Lizzie would never forgive me, if she knew everything I did and had caused. I wouldn't blame her. But here she was, looking at me, so beautiful, so lovely, wanting for me to tell her something. "I guess, for lack of a better word . . . complicated."

"Do you feel like you're in a rut? Too much of a routine?" Lizzie asked.

"No, it's not either of those, I don't think." Maybe, I just really miss you, Lizzie, I thought.

"I think sometimes when we're with someone for a very long time," Lizzie explained, "and I'm only speaking hypothetically, mind you, because I don't and probably never will fall into that category, it might be the relationship can seem stale, worn out. Have you fallen out of love, Daniel?"

"With Jules?"

"Well, yes, who else would I be referring to? Is there someone else?"

A wave of emotion came over me fast and so sudden, I didn't know how to process the feelings. Every single thought I had, now was of Lizzie and what we'd meant to each other over the years. The happiness and joy we shared and experienced. "It's you, Lizzie," I uttered without thinking.

"Excuse me?" Lizzie pulled her hand off my arm and looked at me, searching my face, trying to figure out what was behind my words. "What do you mean, it's me?"

"I didn't realize it until just now. I've never stopped loving you."

Lizzie's body tensed. "Daniel, don't. That was a long time ago, we've both moved on," she reminded me.

"I never should have left you, I'm such a fool. There was no real need to try and find out about the missing piece of my past. It should have stayed buried."

"What are you talking about? You didn't leave me, we broke up, I don't understand what you mean by missing piece of the past? I think you're confusing things."

I shook my head, wondering what the hell it was I was doing. "No, I'm sorry. I'm not, I'm just— don't pay any attention to me, Lizzie. I don't know what's wrong with me. I'm sorry," I said and stood up. "I should probably just get you back to your car now. I've said too much."

Lizzie reached up and pulled me back down so I was, again, sitting beside her. "Hey Daniel, stop," she said softly. "Talk to me."

Lizzie's concerned and soothing voice opened the gates and the tears I had no idea were waiting, began to spill from my eyes. I cried like a baby and reached over and pulled Lizzie to me. She wrapped her arms around me and slowly moved her hands up and down my back.

Steve Wilhelm's: Another Time To Love

"I'm so sorry, Lizzie," I sobbed into her neck. "I never meant—."

"Shh, it's okay, Daniel," Lizzie lulled. "Let it out. You're okay." She held me for a while, until my sobs quieted and I was able to get some control over myself.

I slowly pulled my face back far enough so that I could gaze into her mesmerizing eyes. I could tell Lizzie had been moved by my emotions, as her eyes were moist as well. Her lips were full and barely parted and I couldn't help myself and slowly brought my lips to hers. She didn't pull away and the touch was electric. I could feel her breath catch as our kiss deepened and she reached her hands to my cheeks and caressed lightly. Finally, I pulled away and looked down. "I'm sorry, I didn't mean to do that," I said, wondering why I was suddenly embarrassed.

"I—, I'm . . . surprised you did," Lizzie gasped. Her eyes were shining with light.

"I honestly—" Lizzie brought her finger up and put in on my lips.

"Don't say anything, Daniel could you . . . just do it again, because if you don't, I will!"

She brought her lips back to mine and opened her mouth as we kissed again. Her tongue darted in and out and our teasing tongue-tag sent shivers and goosebumps coursing throughout my body. My manhood was suddenly engorged with blood and felt harder than it had been in a long time. I had to shift on the bench to allow it more room in my pants. I smiled and Lizzie pulled back slightly.

"Why're you smiling," Lizzie asked coyly.

Steve Wilhelm's: Another Time To Love

"Because of the wonderful way you're making me feel right now," I answered. "Energized and manly." Lizzie tip-toed her fingers down my leg, lightly grazing over the tip of my head through my pants, causing me to suddenly suck in my breath. "Oh, my God, Lizzie," I murmured. I didn't want her touch to stop. It felt so right, yet at the same time, it felt taboo and illicit, which made me want her to do it that much more. "What're we doing?" I said as I kissed her under her chin and went up behind her ears. I felt her shudder and her hand pressed into my hardness.

"You remembered . . . how that . . . what that does when you kiss me there . . ." Lizzie panted.

"We're going to get arrested for public indecency if you keep this up," I said against her ear.

"Do you want to stop?" Lizzie asked me. She gently moved her hands up to caress my face.

"No," I said in truth. "I really don't. Do you?"

"Do you want to feel my response to that?" Lizzie. "Feel what your kisses are causing?" She took my hand and started to move it down. I stopped her and smiled.

"I get the picture, seriously," I said. "But maybe we could go somewhere a bit more private?"

"That would be a good start," Lizzie agreed. She slowly stood and brought her purse up against her chest. "Are you coming," She asked when I didn't move.

"Umm, I need to wait a moment or two," I said sheepishly. Lizzie smiled and looked directly at the bulge showing in my pants. She nodded. "You keep staring and

Steve Wilhelm's: Another Time To Love

it will go down, but it'll cause a mess in there," I said. "If you get my meaning . . ."

"Yes, we wouldn't want that to happen, at least not here," Lizzie said, mischievously licking her lips.

"You're making this harder, you know," I said and winced at my unintended pun.

We finally were able to make it back to pick up Lizzie's car. I followed her to her place, which was about ten minutes from downtown Kirkland. She was renting one half of a small, cozy two bedroom duplex in a quaint non-descript neighborhood. It reminded me a little of the place she and I first had in Los Angeles when we first moved in together. Lizzie conducted a quick tour once we were inside and I was impressed with what she'd done with seemingly so little. It felt like a home, though I could sense her slight embarrassment as I knew she was used to better.

"Would you like a glass of white wine?" Lizzie asked.

"Yes I would, thank you," I called back. I definitely could use something to ease the nervousness I felt. She opened the refrigerator and pulled out a bottle with the plain label 'WHITE WINE' on it. I laughed out loud. "I've actually heard that this brand is better because all the money went to the product and not the labels," I commented.

"Yeah, sure." she laughed. "We'll go with that."

We took our glasses and sat next to each other on the couch. There was an awkward silence as we sipped

Steve Wilhelm's: Another Time To Love

the wine and looked around the room. Lizzie got up and turned on the stereo receiver and found a smooth jazz station. "Is that okay?" she asked.

"Of course," I answered. I remembered we used to snuggle together after meals occasionally, sometimes falling asleep in each other's arms listening to jazz. Now, it seemed so long ago.

Lizzie set her glass down on the coffee table and turned to look at me. "Are you as nervous as I am?"

"And here I thought it was just me," I said and pushed my breath out. "I feel like a teenager over at a girl's house for the first time, wondering if I'm going to be able to work up the nerve to make a move, because I really want to make out with you," I admitted.

Lizzie smiled warmly. "Do you remember our first kiss?"

"I do," I said. "The night at that fraternity house party. We caught up with each other out on the back porch, trying to get away from the loud music. We talked for hours and hours, like we had known each other all our lives. Then, I asked you to dance, and it turned into a slow song, remember?"

"I remember wondering how many toes of mine you might injure," Lizzie said laughing.

"I whispered in your ear that I wanted to try something and then I turned your face to mine and kissed you."

"I hadn't expected that, but honestly, I was hoping you would try it."

Steve Wilhelm's: Another Time To Love

"That's when I found out how sensitive behind the ears you are when my kisses took me there."

"As you noted a little earlier, I still am," Lizzie reminded me, lightly caressing my arm. "Daniel, listen. There's something I want to say."

"Okay, sure," I said. I set my own glass on the table.

"Seeing you at the coffee shop the other day and now spending this time with you again has been really good. I hadn't realized how much I'd missed you, how much I still care."

"I know what you're saying," I said. I reached for her hands and she pulled them just out of reach.

"Not yet," Lizzie said. "I know you're hurting a lot right now. I know that what's going on between you and Jules has probably left you questioning lots of things and I understand that. You're undoubtedly very vulnerable, and I don't want you to think I'm trying to take advantage of that. That wouldn't be right. I mean, I . . . do want to be with you, truly in the worst way. I thought a lot about it on the way here from the café, that even if you were to patch things up with Jules tomorrow . . . that I still want you today, in this moment." Lizzie was turning red in the face. "Oh hell, I'm rambling, I'm so freaking nervous," she said and rolled her eyes.

I reached over and stroked her cheek with my finger. Her skin was soft and warm to the touch, I had missed it so much. "Lizzie, I don't know if it's the wine, you, or me, but right now, I feel as if all the awkwardness has lifted and I'm where I need to be. I don't want to think

Steve Wilhelm's: Another Time To Love

about Jules, or anyone else but you," I said. I felt myself becoming aroused once again and it felt good and natural. "You still have a pull over me, I'm not sure you realize that."

"I do?" She searched my face for more answers.

I took her hand and placed it on my chest. "Feel my heartbeat? It's going like a zillion miles an hour." And it was, so much so that it was nearly beating right out of my chest.

"Mine, too," she repeated, moving our hands to her own chest. I could feel her naked breasts through the thin material of her blouse and her nipples were getting hard as pebbles at my touch, making my blood flow even harder.

I leaned closer to say something in her ear. "I want to take you to your bedroom," I whispered.

"Well then shut up and do it," Lizzie whispered back hoarsely.

I stood and picked her up in my arms and carried her to the bedroom, kissing her passionately on the way there. By the time I set her down on the bed, I was so hard with arousal, I was afraid I might blow before anything happened. Lizzie tried to sit up and reach for the front of my jeans. I nudged her back down. "Just relax and let me pamper you. I want to touch, explore and please you first," I said as I sat next to her and started massaging her shoulders. My fingers then began to unbutton her shirt from the top down, slowly and deliberately. I leaned down and kissed her lips as I reached in and cupped her

Steve Wilhelm's: Another Time To Love

breasts, then kneaded her nipples to attention with my fingertips. Lizzie moaned and started to move her hips against me. Her breathing became ragged and short. I opened her shirt up completely and she helped me take it off.

I kissed my way down and around each breast, licking and tasting each soft mound. She reached and toyed with the hair on my head with her fingers, and then began to push so that I could continue my exploration further down her body. I pulled the buttons on her jeans until they popped open and then gently tugged her pants down below her knees. I admired her cute panties with a big red heart covering the front. I licked from the elastic top down to where her lips were barely covered by the silky fabric. I pushed the material inside her folds with my tongue and felt her tense and she inhaled sharply.

"Oh holy shit, Daniel!" she gasped loudly and her body tensed and she pushed herself hard against my mouth. I could taste her juices through her panties and then she sighed and relaxed.

She sat up and we got her jeans and panties all the way off. She reached down and unbuttoned my own pants while I pulled my shirt off over my head. She pulled my jeans and briefs off and tossed them to the floor. With ease, she took hold of my cock and gently stroked the shaft first from the underside and then up and over the tip, causing pre-cum to dribble out. She bent down and took me in her mouth and slowly sucked and moved her tongue around and around, which made my eyes roll back

Steve Wilhelm's: Another Time To Love

into my head. She could tell I was about ready to lose it, but I didn't want to cum yet.

I gently brought her head back up and looked deep into her eyes. "Lizzie, I want you," I said. She smiled, her hands moved down my back to grab my butt and she was pulling on me. I took my cock and placed it at her warm entrance and with a quick gentle push I easily slid all the way in. Her pussy muscles gripped my shaft, alternating between squeezing and letting loose. Lizzie was breathing hard against my neck and I could hear her saying "My God, my God, I'm going to cum!" and at that, I swelled up and came deep inside. I lost count of my contractions and finally was spent. Lizzie was lost in her own orgasm and held me tight, almost squeezing the breath out of me. She suddenly relaxed and opened her eyes, tears starting to collect.

"Daniel, I haven't cum like that probably ever before," she looked at me and kissed me deeply.

"I don't think I have either," I said, truthfully.

"I want to again," she said.

Who was I to say no?

"How could any man in his right mind ever cheat on you?" I asked as I lightly stroked the warm skin of her back. We lay on the bed together, enjoying the naked intimacy of after our lovemaking. "You're so completely arousing. Beautiful, sensual . . . I could go on and on."

"And I wouldn't stop you," she said with a smile. She sighed and stretched. "I don't know. I guess some only see

Steve Wilhelm's: Another Time To Love

what they want to. They do what they want, take what they want and if they don't get what they want, they lash out." Lizzie turned over onto her back and reached over, running her fingers through my chest hairs. "Thank you for your compliments. I could never tire of hearing them from you," she said.

I propped my head up with one hand and looked at Lizzie's perfect body. Her nipples were still hard from arousal, poking up at the ceiling. It caused a stirring in my groin. "What do we do now?" I wondered out loud.

"I think the best thing is to take it one day at a time," she said. "I can't think of any place better I'd rather be right now, but at the same time, I wouldn't want to risk complicating your life any more than it already seems to be."

"Honestly, I don't think you could," I said.

"I'm just sayin . . ." Lizzie added. Her hand moved down and absently fondled my semi-erection. "We need to find the off switch for this, because I need to get ready for work." She squeezed me gently and then sat up in bed.

"You have another job?" I asked, not really surprised.

"I'm the evening hostess at *Anthony's Home Port*," Lizzie explained.

"Classy restaurant," I commented. "Excellent seafood. I've eaten there a time or two."

"And they do treat me well there," Lizzie said. "I've been able to start saving some extra money for things."

"I'm happy for you," I offered. I stood and found my shirt which had been thrown across the room. "I'd like to

Steve Wilhelm's: Another Time To Love

see you again," I told her as I put it on. I saw Lizzie was still staring at me below the belt. "Hey!" I said. "My eyes are up here," I pointed at my face and laughed. I ducked as she threw her panties at me playfully.

Lizzie then buttoned my shirt up for me and I watched her, wishing we didn't have to part. "I want to see you, too," Lizzie said, softly. "But you know you need to get things figured out, Daniel." She was right, I thought.

"I know. Believe me, the last thing I want is to cause new problems or strife in your life, either. You deserve the best and I mean that."

"Well, don't go selling yourself short, by any means," Lizzie said. "You deserve the best and more, too."

I wanted to enjoy getting soapy and wet in the shower with Lizzie, but she spiritedly declined, as we both knew she would end up very late if not completely absent from work if we did. I put the rest of my clothes on and wrapped my arms around her in a warm bear hug, kissing her lips tenderly for a moment and then let her go. "Have a good night at work Lizzie," I said.

"I will, thank you, Daniel," she told me. She gave me a quick kiss and walked me towards the door. "Drive careful and call me over the weekend. Let me know how things are going." She blew me a kiss as I walked out and I turned to watch the door close behind me. As I walked to my car, I had the biggest smile permanently written on my face, like a kid who just found out he could eat all the Halloween candy in his bag for dinner. However, as happy as I felt, I did think it would be prudent to rein it in just a

Steve Wilhelm's: Another Time To Love

bit. Nothing had changed except finding out I was not stricken with impotence after all. That was a huge relief.

Steve Wilhelm's: Another Time To Love

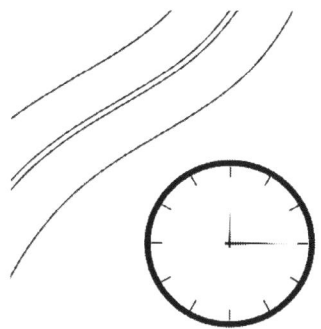

CHAPTER EIGHT

"I won't suggest you did anything wrong," Jeff pointed out after thinking over what I told him about my day with Lizzie. "I mean, you were married to her after all, so that has to be taken into consideration, right?"

"Exactly. That's what I was thinking," I said. "Making love with Lizzie felt so natural, so right. It's really made me miss what she and I had." I walked over to the refrigerator and got out a bottled water. I was parched after all the exercise Lizzie and I had earlier. I sat down at the kitchen table and drank over half the bottle before setting it down in front of me.

"Here's something I thought about today," Jeff said. "We pretty much know the effects of your changes on most of us, because we know how they were before, but we really don't know anything about Jules' past. I'm only bringing this up in case it might help you in your deciding on what you want to do."

Steve Wilhelm's: Another Time To Love

"Okay, I'm all ears," I said, I wasn't doing any good making my own decisions. Just getting myself into more trouble.

He sat down across from me at the table. "Think about this. Who is the only person you didn't know anything about before you began this adventure?"

"Well, that would be Jules, of course."

"Right. She was the unknown, she was taken from the original timeline. For all we know, in her timeline, she could have been married, she could have gone on a mission to preach religion deep in the jungles of the Amazon, she could have been murdered in the streets of Tijuana, Mexico a year after high school. We just don't know. The point is, she was removed from the path that she was supposed to be on." How was he able to make more sense of this than me? Needless to say, I'd be lost without Jeff.

"Sure, but so was everyone else," I replied. "What makes her any different from the others?"

"Good question. Now that you asked that, I kind of lost the importance of where I was going," Jeff joked, laughing lightly. "Maybe wherever Jules was, whatever she was doing, maybe that would have had significant effect on the world and now it won't." Now the cogwheels were turning.

"Oh, like on this 'mission in the Amazon,' she might have discovered the cure for cancer? Or, something like that?"

Steve Wilhelm's: Another Time To Love

"Yes! Now you're seeing it!" Jeff sounded excited at my realization.

"So, playing devil's advocate, what if by saving you from dying of your own cancer, you then invented the newest and greatest alternative to the materials golf clubs are made of. You found a cheaper, more efficient way to manufacture them and ultimately reduce the expense of clubs for all the golfers around the world and became a millionaire!" Just what had I done to the world? If this were possible, could I be the only one?

"The point is, that wasn't my original destiny. That outcome wasn't supposed to be." Jeff stood and gazed out the kitchen window at the approaching darkness that seemed to grow darker even still. Gripping the faucet handle, turned on the sink and washed his hands. "I still believe that the universe will ultimately do what needs to be done to realign the paths of everyone affected. Yours as well."

"So basically, my hands are tied no matter what I do. . ." I trailed off.

"Perhaps," Jeff affirmed. "I don't have a degree in this field and for all we know, I could be speaking out of my ass with this entire conversation." He shrugged his shoulders.

"I'm exhausted and really need to let my brain rest. A lot's been happening this week and I need to process," I acknowledged, pushing away from the table. I paused for a moment and looked at Jeff, suddenly curious. "Do you think that if I went back and was successful in stopping

Steve Wilhelm's: Another Time To Love

myself from doing what I did, and things went back to the way they were . . . would you miss anything from now? Would you resent me in any way?"

"I'd be dead, Daniel," Jeff answered simply. "How could I miss what didn't happen? I'm sure I would be smiling down upon you from Heaven and giving you a high five for doing the right thing!"

"Yeah, good point," I agreed. "Keep that optimism of yours about Heaven. I would hope I'd end up there when my time is up and not find myself in the other place, if you know where I mean." I haven't exactly been the most honest guy lately.

"Go to bed, Daniel," Jeff basically commanded in a soft tone. "We'll chat more in the morning."

I wasn't as surprised as he thought I'd be when he told me after breakfast that he was going to go in to work. He said that a shipment of new golf slacks had arrived, and he really needed to be there to insure the quality was up to his standards. After all, his name was on them, so he had to put his own stamp of approval on them, too. I completely understood, he didn't have to explain.

I told Jeff of my decision to go back and see Mathew and convince him to send me back to where I belonged. He said he'd be anxious to hear about that when we both were back for dinner. He wished me luck and we both left without saying much more. I think we both knew our friendship, as it was, would soon end. I sat in the waiting room for however long it took to see Mathew. His

Steve Wilhelm's: Another Time To Love

receptionist said that since I hadn't made an appointment, she would have a hard time fitting me in, but she might be able to squeeze me in between appointments. I told her that would be fine, that I didn't have anywhere to be right away.

I looked at my watch and saw it had only been an hour since I sat down and made myself comfortable in the waiting room. Not too bad, I thought. I had seen a few people show up to be taken back immediately and I could only hope he had another patient no show, or cancel. I was patient, but as I looked at my foot twitching as if it had a life of its own, it obviously had other ideas. I willed it to stop, unsuccessfully, so I let twitch away. What was it that had led me to my decision? After careful consideration, I decided it was ultimately seeing all that had happened to Lizzie. She had a successful and wonderful life prior to my blundering move. Since I had not been there in the long run, she had met that loser who had abused her and her trust. That snowballed into repercussions and, because of me, her career that she had worked so long and hard to build, had been taken away from her as if she never deserved it. She is such a fighter and a survivor, I thought smiling proudly. She certainly never ran away and sank to the bottom of her personal well to give up. Not Lizzie, but she shouldn't have to be working this hard, having to be at two jobs to barely make ends meet? She was putting up a façade, but I knew she was miserable.

Steve Wilhelm's: Another Time To Love

I saw how the time we spent together since we ran into each other at the coffee shop, meant something to her. It meant everything to me, I absolutely am certain of that. It showed me what I had left behind, and I believe that it showed her what a different future could have held for her. The future she couldn't know she once already lived. I took that away and at that moment of clarity last night as my sorry brain was processing all this information, I knew. Whatever I had to do, however I had to do it, I had to somehow go back and stop myself from seeing Mathew the first time.

"Daniel Allen?" I heard a robust woman's voice call after me. "If you would, please come with me."

I brought my thoughts back to the here and now and stood. I followed the receptionist as she led me to a room down the hallway. She opened the door and allowed me to enter past her. "Thank you," I offered.

"The doctor will be in to see you in a moment," the nurse replied with and left, leaving me to wait again.

I gazed around the softly lit room, simply decorated with a small table coming out from the wall and a chair on either side. A picture in a frame on the wall on the opposite side was hanging next to a certificate of some sort. This must be the consult room, and not the regular room I thought he would use. It was not at all what I remembered from before, but that wasn't surprising.

Then, there was a light knock at the door and it opened. Mathew came in the room and held out his hand. "Good morning, I'm Dr. Mathew Stevens." I reached out

Steve Wilhelm's: Another Time To Love

and took his hand and shock it. His grip was firm, but pleasant.

"Hello Dr. Stevens," I answered. "Daniel Allen."

He closed the door and sat down at the table and I followed suit, sitting down across from him. "My receptionist said you were very anxious to see me, have we met before?" He asked curiously.

"Yes," I said hesitantly. I had decided before that I should be more direct than ambiguous. "I'm not sure you'll remember me, but we *have* met previously."

Mathew looked at me more intensely, and I could tell he was racking his brain to recall having encountered me before. Then, there was a glimmer of recollection, faint, but I was sure I saw it in his eyes. "You do seem familiar, though I can't seem to place when or where," he commented. "I must apologize, as I usually have a better memory than this." The doctor blinked a few extra times, clearly allowing his brain to search for the missing information it needed.

"I'm glad you have even a little sense of familiarity, because I know what I'm about to tell you will seem quite unbelievable. I wouldn't be at all offended if after listening, you tell me to go take a flying leap, or that you feel I'm so totally full of shit, that there's not a shovel big enough to dig me out." I cleared my throat, surprised at my forwardness. I was done playing games with time.

"Interesting way to start out a conversation, I must say, but now you do have my undivided attention. Please, by all means…continue," Mathew spilled out.

Steve Wilhelm's: Another Time To Love

"Thank you. It would do well to suspend any current notions on . . . well, no," I stopped. That wasn't the way to go, I thought. "Just hear me out and I'll do my best to explain anything that you will undoubtedly have questions on."

"Fair enough," Mathew expressed.

"I don't remember exactly when, because my perception of time has been permanently skewed, but you and I met at a tavern in town one afternoon. I was there, because I had been thrown for a loop after realizing I couldn't remember what had happened to my old high school girlfriend. It was drew me absolutely insane. You were there because you were distraught over the loss of your research partner, Alex. He had been involved in a fatal car accident and you told me they had just taken him off life support." I watched Mathew's reactions as I spoke. He nodded occasionally, but gave no indication of whether what I was saying had actually occurred in this time line, or not.

"Anyway," I continued, "You bought me a refill of what I was drinking and we talked and after I told you more about my issue, you told me about the project you were working on and convinced me to be a test subject. As though it would benefit both of us."

"I see," Mathew revealed.

"Is any of this making any sense?" I asked, praying my words weren't making me look insane. "Or, would you like me wait while you call someone to take me to the looney bin."

Steve Wilhelm's: Another Time To Love

"I would like you to go on," Mathew suggested. "And... then I will tell you my thoughts."

That wasn't quite the response I was expecting, I thought. It was more equivocal than not, but he left me the floor to continue.

"Ultimately, your goal and mine, was to enable me to go back and find out what happened in my past, learn that which I could not remember and then I could move on. Of course, being an untested procedure, and therefore the outcome was unknown, we had no idea that I could interact when I was back in my high school body and I did what you had warned me not to do. I got caught up in my old life of twenty plus years in the past and seeing my girlfriend who had disappeared. It was overwhelming. I couldn't control myself and ended up changing what had happened in the past. Which, as you can guess, has changed and really screwed up my present. Well, let me amend that. It's messed up more than just my life. It seems everyone I know has been affected to some degree."

Mathew put up a hand and gestured for me to stop. "So correct me if I'm wrong, but now you would like me to send you back so that you can set your path back to the way it was previously?"

"Uh well...basically, yes," I stammered.

"This is fascinating, your story," Mathew nodded his head. He looked at his hands as he thought for a long moment. I was feeling a little anxious wondering what he was going to say.

Steve Wilhelm's: Another Time To Love

"And…you think I'm six eggs short of a dozen," I interjected, gearing up to stand. "I'm sorry to have wasted your time."

"Nonsense," Mathew said. "Please, sit back down. I don't disbelieve you at all. There are basic truths to what you have told me. I've been working on a theoretical procedure to enable those who suffer from memory loss to seek out what they are looking for. It is true, that I have a research partner named Alex. No one would know that unless I had told them. No one would know any of this without knowledge from me, in fact. I will tell you that Alex *was* involved in a car accident, but thankfully he survived."

"I'm getting the feeling that you might actually believe me," I said.

"As I mentioned, you do seem extremely familiar. I can't say definitively why, but yes, I do believe you." And there it was, a glimmer of hope that I never expected.

"So, you've been affected by my changes as well, or . . . I guess Alex has, being that he is alive and well," I pondered.

"I'm very pleased that my procedure apparently was a success. Well, not in the sense of what you have experienced, but the fact that we're able to send you back to remember your past, I mean. You must tell me more about this. Can you enlighten me on any details of what you remember about the procedure?"

"Only that you had electrodes hooked up to me to monitor heart rates, and such. You injected me with some

Steve Wilhelm's: Another Time To Love

kind of serum you said would work with my brain to enhance certain regions and facilitate, or stimulate what was necessary."

"Yes, I know what you're referring to. Excellent," Mathew reacted, raising his brow.

I shook my head in amazement and replied, "I'm just floored."

"Why's that?" He queried.

"I thought this whole interaction would go in a completely different direction," I eagerly told him. "I mean, here I am, practically a total stranger to you, raving about something that most would think was out of some dime store time-travel novel. But, you pretty much without batting an eye, take me at my word, no questions asked." I almost couldn't believe it.

"True, but you have one thing going in your favor," Mathew explained. "I highly doubt that anyone would take the time and effort to make up such a tale and then risk coming to me, of all people, if there wasn't something more behind the story. You display no signs of deception. I could tell that by your demeanor, how you reacted while telling me your side of the story. And... the whole thing is theoretically possible. So again, yes, I believe you."

"Will you help me then?" I asked, almost holding my breath.

"If I said no, I might regret it for the rest of my life," he admitted. "I've had to put my research on the side burner as of the last half a year or so, due to other commitments,

Steve Wilhelm's: Another Time To Love

but I think this will be of benefit to us both, don't you agree, Daniel?"

"Yes, I do," I managed to put together, breathing out easier. "Thank you so very much Dr. Stevens. You have no idea how relieved I am at hearing you say those words."

"Please, Daniel, call me Mathew," he offered. "I would like to move forward on this sooner, rather than later. If you wouldn't be opposed it, of course. Can you free up Monday for me? I'll be able to prepare things over the weekend for our experiment."

"Holy shit," I exclaimed, almost reeling in my words as they came out. I was trying to maintain a level of somewhat respectability.

"Will that be a problem," he asked me.

"No, I just wasn't expecting any of this. I am happy to do what's needed for the both of us."

"Excellent, excellent," Mathew expressed as he rose from his chair at the table. "Daniel, I'm looking forward to us working together. I think it's fate that has brought you back to me at this time, and we shouldn't let this opportunity pass us by. For, if you think about it...we didn't allow this tremendous opportunity to slip us by in the past, why should we in the future? It's the only way out of this unpleasant situation."

"Trust me, Dr. S— I mean, Mathew...I doubt there's anything that'll stop me from making our appointment. I just want everything to go back to normal and live out the rest of my life as it was before. I'm just sorry I didn't listen to your advice the first time."

Steve Wilhelm's: Another Time To Love

"Not to worry, Daniel. I learned a long time ago, that there is a reason for everything that happens. So, let's move forward now."

I stood up and we shook hands. I may have squeezed a little tighter than was warranted, but I was excited to have my life back. "What time Monday?" I inquired.

"Let's make it ten, that all right?" He proposed.

"Ten a.m. it is," I agreed.

I beamed as I power walked to my car. Ever since seeing Lizzie again, things had taken a turn for the better. I crossed my fingers that things would continue toward making things right.

***

I finished telling Jeff about my meeting with Mathew. He, of course, nodded his head in approval. "I think under the circumstances, it's probably the best choice to make," he said. "And Mathew, well, I've never met the guy . . . have I?"

"No, I don't think you have, in any timeline," I answered.

"He sounds like a good stand-up guy. From the way the conversation went, he does seem to be upfront and honest. I think he very well may be able to help you. I mean, if the procedure works and everything. That's just my gut feeling."

"Thank you," I told him. "Your belief and support means everything to me, but I know that's something I've

Steve Wilhelm's: Another Time To Love

told you a million times. I truly mean it. I'd be in a bad spot without you, Jeff."

"Of course," Jeff smiled back. "It's how we roll." I knew I could count on him to lighten the mood.

I yawned. "I bet I sleep soundly tonight."

"I think we should just order a pizza," Jeff suggested. "I can't remember when I got so old that the weekend nights felt no different than any other night. I swear, when it gets any later than seven in the evening, I seriously start thinking about how nice it would be to go to bed early! What's wrong with me?" He mused.

"I can say, it's not just you," I said with a laugh. "I've been like that for years!"

"So, what're you going to do about Jules and Maggie?" Jeff wondered.

"I thought about that earlier, as I was driving back from Mathew's office," I said. "I guess I'll do my best to patch things up with Jules over the weekend. If nothing else, I'll feel better about myself that I tried. Maggie? I just want to find out what the heck is making her ditch school and come back home. Oh, and thank you for reminding me. I need to call Jules and find out when she wants me over there, because Maggie is already home. I think she thinks Maggie will talk if both she and I confront her."

"Sure, just like that show where each week a family gets an intervention going for a family member. I got it. That might be effective, and again, it could backfire. How

Steve Wilhelm's: Another Time To Love

well did you ever respond when confronted by both your mom and dad together?"

"Best answer is, I never did anything to cause confrontations. Having said that, I think I would be rebellious if they had tried. Go against anything they were talking about." I stopped and thought, a smile spreading over my face. "Just like I'm sure Maggie will do. She can be the stubborn child when she wants to be!"

"Takes more after Jules than you, I would venture to say," Jeff commented.

"I can't disagree with you there," I said. I pulled out my wallet and grabbed a couple of twenty dollar bills. I gave them to Jeff. "Tell you what. You order the pizza, anything on it you want. Just make sure there's no fishy stuff on it. I need to go make a call."

"Roger that," Jeff exclaimed.

I left the kitchen and headed to the guest bedroom to make the call.

"Hey Jules," I acknowledged when I heard her answer.

"Hi Daniel, how are you doing?" Jules surprised me by sounding civil.

"I'm doing okay, I've done a lot of thinking over the week, and I really would look forward to talking with you. I think things are going to be okay."

"I've missed you, too," Jules said. "Part of me has been wondering if I was too rash in telling you to leave, but if being apart has somehow made a difference, then maybe it was a good thing."

Steve Wilhelm's: Another Time To Love

"The time has definitely helped me to be able to work on putting things in perspective," I said.

"I'd like you to come over tonight, so that we can talk to Maggie together," Jules disclosed.

"Let's stick to the plan and I'll come by the house tomorrow morning. Will ten be too early?"

"Oh," Jules sounded a little surprised. "Okay, I guess that will work."

"How is Maggie? Has she said anything about why she came back?"

"She's Maggie," Jules said. "She's done everything in her power to avoid talking about that particular subject. You're good with her, I would wager a lot that you'd be able to get her to tell us."

I laughed. "Sure, we can play good cop, bad cop."

"Hmm, that sounds fun and how will we handle Maggie, then?" I heard Jules giggle, though I could tell she was trying to suppress it. "Oh, you mean that'll be our tactic with Maggie, I gotcha."

I smiled to myself. It sounded like Jules was in a much better place. She was quite a bit more playful than I'd heard her in quite a while. "Be careful love, you might be starting something you can't finish."

"Now, Danny," Jules uttered. "You know I always finish what I start."

"Good point," I said. "Okay, I'll see you both in the morning. Sleep well."

I pressed the disconnect button. That went too well, I thought. I need to touch bases with Lizzie and see if I can

Steve Wilhelm's: Another Time To Love

see her Sunday evening. I really would like to spend some time with her before I go. I feel it's right to be with her and reassure her that things will be okay. Strangely, I feel quite calm. I feel good, like I'm heading towards a new beginning. I just need to connect with those important to me once more, especially the people I won't see alive again.

Don't worry, Mom, I thought. I'll make the time to see you, too. You won't get away from me again that easily.

Though our phone call seemed completely positive and upbeat, the hug Jules and I gave each other when I arrived at the house was rather awkward. It was understandably so, and I didn't think much of it. I didn't push for a kiss, and Jules didn't either, so it was okay. I didn't have any experience in separations with spouses, but it seemed normal enough, due to the circumstances. I wasn't going to stress over it.

I followed her into the living room and sat down on the couch while she went to get Maggie. I had to smile as the whole thing felt just like an intervention. I just didn't have a clue as to what we were going to intervene with.

"Mom, do we *have* to do this," I heard Maggie's voice as the girls came into the room. My daughter came over to me and gave me a quick hug along with a kiss on the cheek. "Hi, Daddy," she said to me. "Are you moving back home now?"

Steve Wilhelm's: Another Time To Love

"He's here to talk with you and me, Maggie," Jules said before I could answer for myself. "We can talk about that later."

"Oh, geez," Maggie wailed dramatically, rolling her eyes. "What's the big deal, Mom? I just needed some time away from school. There are a few things I needed to take care of."

"Sweetie, personally, I don't think it's much like you at all to do something like this," I opened up with. "Usually, you dig right in and make the best of things. You don't run away. You never have." Jules looked at me and nodded in agreement. I smiled and then saw something else in her eyes. I could swear that she knew something more.

"Actually, I'm not running away from anything," Maggie said.

"Well, what is it then?" Jules asked.

Maggie looked at Jules for a moment and then I saw her eyes go wide. "You already know, don't you Mom?"

"I'm a mother," Jules reminded her. "I can tell. You'll know the same when you have children, trust me. You'll be the same way."

"All right," I said, sitting up on the couch looking from Jules to Maggie. "It appears I'm the only one who knows nothing about what's going on. Would either of you care to share with old pops here?"

"Um . . . Daddy," Maggie looked at me, her face getting red and she fidgeted a little, shifting her feet from side to side.

Steve Wilhelm's: Another Time To Love

"It's okay, Maggie," I said. "Whatever it is, it can't be as bad as all that, can it? No matter what, I'll love you without judgement."

Maggie breathed out and smiled weakly. "Okay, well . . . Daddy, I'm pregnant."

"Your . . . pregnant?" I repeated, very astonished. I looked over at Jules and she nodded her head slightly. "Oh, shit," I said, under my breath, but I knew Maggie heard me. She looked down at the floor and I could tell she was about to cry. "Maggie, I'm sorry, that's not what I meant to say. What you said is . . . well, it just took me completely by surprise." I hadn't had any time to process this information, unlike Jules. Maggie slowly walked over and sat down next to me on the couch and reached over and hugged me. I put my arms around her and returned the affection. I smiled as Jules also joined us, sitting down next to Maggie on the other side of her.

"What I would like to know, is what we're going to do about this situation," Jules commented. It wasn't meant to be a mean degrading tone of voice, but rather matter of fact. Although, I could see the look of disappointment in Jules' eyes.

"What are _we_ going to do about it?" I asked. "I think we need to be supportive of our daughter, first of all."

"She's going to need more than just our support," Jules added.

"And we'll be there for her, whatever she needs," I said.

Steve Wilhelm's: Another Time To Love

"Guys," Maggie interjected. "I'm right here you know?"

"I'm sorry, you're right," I gave in. "I apologize for not respecting that."

"He's right," Jules said. "Who's the father? Is it that boy Alan? It is, isn't it. Does he know?" Her questions were like rapid gunfire.

"Mom," Maggie said gruffly. "Does it really matter? I really didn't want to involve you guys in this. It's my problem, I got myself into. If it really makes a difference, then yes, it is Alan, he's the father. Does he know? No, he doesn't. I really wanted to tell him when I came back for Daddy, but it never seemed like the right time."

"How long have you known," I asked.

"A couple of weeks, I don't know," Maggie answered. "I don't even know why I should tell him about it. Maybe so he can decide if he wants to be there with me when I go to have the abortion."

I wasn't really listening, because I started to think how wonderful it was going to be being a grandfather. Being able to spoil the child rotten and do all the things we used to do when Maggie was little. Then, that word hit me that Maggie had used. *Abortion*. The warm fuzzy feeling that was just about to envelope me disappeared faster than a snowflake in the Sahara Desert. "Abortion? That seems...so final, you know? Have you considered alternatives? Like adoption?"

Steve Wilhelm's: Another Time To Love

"Daniel, she's too young to have a baby right now. I think she's making the right choice," Jules jumped in and stated.

"Maybe Alan might think differently," I countered. "Have you considered that, Maggie?"

"Mom's right, Daddy. Yes, I've thought about adoption, and I think if I were to carry the baby to term and give birth, I highly doubt I'd be able to give the baby up at all." Maggie wiped a tear that had fallen on her cheek. "Alan will understand when I tell him. I'm sure he'll be there for me. He's a good guy."

Jules put a reassuring hand on Maggie's arm. "I'm proud of you, honey," she said.

"I'm not very proud of myself right now," Maggie muttered, then stood up. "Look guys, I've made up my mind. I've weighed the pros and cons and I know what I'm doing. I do want to have children, maybe more than one, but just not right now."

"Did you guys use— " I started and then held my tongue.

"Of course we did, Daddy," Maggie curtly cut me off. "I'm sorry, I didn't mean to snap, but people always assume that whenever there's an unexpected pregnancy. I like to think I'm careful, as I was taught to be. You both instilled in me from the very first sex talk we had about how important the use of protection during sex is, unless one is married. These days, who wouldn't follow that rule?"

Steve Wilhelm's: Another Time To Love

Me, I thought, now remembering the other evening with Lizzie. Could this happen to me and Lizzie? My hands suddenly felt clammy. "How about if you just think on it one more night, can we do that? When were you planning on having the, uh . . . abortion," I asked. Just saying the word was difficult for me.

"Monday morning at ten," Maggie said. "I'll think about things before then, but I'm sure I'll be left with the same solution. Please, don't be upset Daddy. I know how great a grandfather you would be, but trust me, you'll get your chance. I promise."

I thought back to when Jules told me years ago that she had had Maggie out of wedlock and wondered if she would feel any different about what Maggie was going to do if she remembered that. Maybe, she wouldn't since that happened in the reality where she had been killed. Who knows what the circumstances were in this current reality. "I'd be lying if I said I won't be sad, but you are an adult and I have to respect your decision," I told her.

Truthfully, I didn't think it would matter too much when I went back and stopped myself from ever going back in the first place. Why did things have to be so damn complicated?

"Thank you both for understanding," Maggie replied. "Now, if we're done, I really need to call Alan." She gave us both a kiss and then left the room, leaving Jules and I alone.

Steve Wilhelm's: Another Time To Love

I took a deep breath and felt some relief now that the confrontation was over. She moved over so she was sitting right next to me.

"How was I?" She asked.

"How were you? What do you mean?"

"You know, did I play the part correctly? The bad cop?" Jules winked and grinned widely.

I laughed and shook my head. "Well, that'll explain how you were acting, all stoic and curt and all. But, you almost gave it away by agreeing right along with what Maggie was saying."

"And you were so very understanding and nice," Jules commented. She took my hand in hers and squeezed it. "The perfect good cop. She opened right up to you, just like I told you she would."

"I guess I have the right touch," I gloated.

"I wholeheartedly agree with that statement," Jules said coyly.

What's gotten into Jules, I wondered. Last night on the phone and now this morning? She's giddy and silly and totally unexpected.

"How've you been, Danny? You look really great! Like you've been resting and not partying or drinking." Jules nodded appreciatively.

"I feel good," I said. "I've been doing a lot of thinking, soul searching about how things have been between us. I don't know that I can put into exact words the reason for all that's happened, but I can tell you that I'm going to be making some changes."

Steve Wilhelm's: Another Time To Love

"Changes? Good changes?"

"Yes, for the better. Changes that will be beneficial for all of us."

"I'm really happy to hear that," Jules said. She leaned in and kissed my cheek. "I've really missed you, Danny." She kissed my other cheek. "I've been so cold sleeping alone in that big, huge bed every night, without you." She kissed the side of my mouth. "All alone. Without you." She kissed me full on the lips, slowly and sensually. I felt her tongue pushing and then finding its way into my mouth.

I kissed back, playing tongue tag with her for a few minutes, enjoying the moment. If she was trying to get me worked up and in the mood for romance, she was succeeding with flying colors. My blood was flowing in every direction, ending up down below and causing an intense erection. Jules then pulled me close to her and I could feel her breasts against my chest. She was worked up, as I could feel her nipples poking out. Were bras a thing of the past? First Lizzie, now Jules. I almost broke out in laughter, but I knew Jules wouldn't appreciate my thoughts. She let her hands wander over my body to felt my hardness.

"Oh, look what I've gone and caused," she exclaimed. "I'm being bad, aren't I? Maybe you'll have to pull out your badge and arrest me, officer." She squeezed me through my jeans. I literally had to stifle a moan.

"Maybe I should," I said in agreement. "But I'm pretty sure the jail is quite overcrowded. Too many bad people.

Steve Wilhelm's: Another Time To Love

It wouldn't be pretty. Haven't you read all the nasty things that happen to people that go to the jailhouse?"

"Then, just take me to bed," she whispered. "I want you to move back, move back home now and make love to me, Danny."

"Jules," I started. My brain was fighting with my body and I wasn't sure which was going to be victorious. I hadn't planned on anything more than dealing with Maggie and then talking with Jules. Sex had honestly been the farthest thing from my thoughts. As great as it sounded, and knowing my cock was fully engorged and wanting its freedom and a release, I felt I had to put a stop to things. It just wouldn't be right, I thought. I had just made love with Lizzie just a few days prior, and jumping right back into bed with Jules, my wife, after that didn't set well with me. Even that thought sounded so wrong. They were both my wives, at one time or another, depending on the timeline. But, I couldn't see having my cake and eating it too. It was just so complicated, and here I was with Jules and she was practically begging me to be with her. I should be exhilarated! Instead, I sat up and as gently as I could, extracted myself from Jules' advances. "Honey, my love, I beg of you not to take this the wrong way. I'm going to kick myself later for doing this, but I think we should wait."

"Did I do something wrong?" She asked with a pout.

"Goodness, no," I admitted. "Quite the contrary. It should be rather evident you did nothing wrong, based on what you just felt. I just feel it might be prudent to take

Steve Wilhelm's: Another Time To Love

things slower. Not rush back in, you know? I honestly can't even believe I'm hearing myself say this, but does it make sense? Besides, with Maggie here and all . . . it might make it awkward."

"No, it doesn't make sense," Jules started, looking slightly peeved. "Well, maybe it does." Jules studied my face for a moment, almost as if seeing me in a new light. "Actually, I kind of like this new you, Daniel. You seem so much more assertive. You've got this air of . . . I don't know . . . authority, that I haven't seen in you for many years. That in itself is a huge turn on for me!"

"It's part of my wanting to make things better, Jules," I said.

"All right then, Mister," Jules said finally. "But you better be ready to make up for the fact that I'm extremely hot, horny and even more worked up than ever before. I need to go stand under a very cold shower, thank you very much. Would you care to join me? I'd bet you a vacation in Tahiti that you need one as much as I do." She looked me square in the groin.

"Tahiti? What about Scotland, or Ireland?" I asked. "In any event, that would totally defeat the purpose of me not taking you to the bedroom right now, wouldn't you think?"

"Perhaps," Jules sulked as she stood. "You'd better go before I decide to go bad cop on you. Don't go off and party all weekend before coming back. I want you fresh and ready to show me how much you love me."

Steve Wilhelm's: Another Time To Love

"I do love you, Jules," I said, standing up from the couch myself.

"I know, and I love you, too," she purred. "Would you humor me with one more kiss before you go?" Before I could answer, she was back in my arms once again. She kissed me deep and forcefully, and obviously did not want me to forget what I was giving up by leaving. "Are you sure you don't want a taste of me to remember what you will be coming back to?" She ground herself against my erection.

"You know I would like nothing better," I said. "But—."

Jules pushed me away gently. "Yeah, I know, I know. Go on, get out of here," she said with a smirk. Jules turned away and left the room, fanning her face as she sauntered out of view.

***

"Mom, you've outdone yourself, once again," I boasted. "Thank you for a wonderful lunch. How do you always manage to put together a feast like this on such short notice?" I had called Mom after leaving Jules to ask if she had time to see me.

"Well, you're just being kind, trying to butter up an old broad," Mom cooed. "And... it's working! It wasn't all that, though. You know that, but thank you for the compliment, Daniel." Mom took the plates to the sink and then came back to sit across from me at the table. She smoothened out the table cloth and set her hands down

Steve Wilhelm's: Another Time To Love

on the table. "Okay, what say we leave the small talk behind and you tell me why you're really here."

Mom was never one to mince words. "You're right. I did have an ulterior motive," I divulged. "It's something I wanted to talk about the last time I was here, but we kind of got sidetracked with my personal issues. Having said that, I can tell you that things are beginning to get much better now that we've had some time off, as it were." I swallowed the remaining saliva in my mouth pretty hard.

"That's good, honey," Mom said, looking rather pleased.

"So, I've had a lot of time to think over my problems and the things I've done to cause them. I believe I know what I can do to set them right," I said and paused.

"Is it safe to say there's really more to everything than just the fight you and Jules had?" Mom asked.

"Yeah, I'm afraid so. That's merely the tip of the iceberg."

"I'm sorry to hear that." The expression on her face gradually dropped.

"I appreciate that Mom, more than you know. You've always had an open mind, right?" I breathed in and out evenly, deciding how best to tell her the truth about things. It was now or never to open up and come clean.

"Well, yes, of course," Mom answered. "Even if you were to tell me you think you were abducted by aliens last year, and you were serious, I would believe you . . . it's nothing like that, is it?"

Steve Wilhelm's: Another Time To Love

"No, that would be a little crazy, don't you think?" Yeah, I thought, that would be crazy, but time travel wouldn't? I almost laughed. "All right, I'm going to do the best I can to tell you, but just listen and then when I'm done, you can ask all the questions you want, as I'm sure you'll have a few."

"Okay, agreed," Mom nodded.

"You mentioned when I was so enthusiastic the last time I was here and said it was so good to see you that it was a little bit of a déjà vu. Well, I can explain to you why."

"Oh?" She hummed curiously.

"I have mentioned that before," I said and recalled with Mom the morning Jules came over for breakfast.

Mom nodded her head. "Goodness, this sounds as if it could get complicated."

"I know," I told her. "Just bear with me. Before you woke me up that morning, I was in a psychotherapist's office participating in an experimental procedure to go back to my past. I was not in the present as you and I are living in right now. It's a difficult concept to explain, as I'm sure it is to hear, believe me." I watched Mom's face and she was listening without judging, nodding for me to continue. "I was married, of course, but to Lizzie, not Jules. You may remember her as Betty, but anyway, I was going through boxes in the garage looking for photos so I could make a DVD photo album to surprise Lizzie and Megan while they were gone. I was going through my high school yearbook and a card from Jules fell out and I then

Steve Wilhelm's: Another Time To Love

realized I had no memory of what happened to her. So, I met this doctor... and long story short, he sent me back into the body of my younger self so I could remember what happened."

"You're serious about this, aren't you?" Mom queried.

"Yes," I stated. "I'm taking the chance of sharing what you might not believe, but I needed to be honest."

"Why do you look at it that way? Taking a chance?"

"Because if you didn't believe me and thought I was making it all up, it could change our relationship that has survived the test of time and my stupidity."

"I don't think that will happen, son," Mom said and reached across the table to touch my hand with hers. "I love you no matter what. I will always believe what you tell me because as I've told you before, you never lie to me, especially about the important things."

I squeezed her hand. "Thank you, Mom. I was advised not to change anything, to merely spectate and learn what happened to Jules, but you remember how I was in those days, always pushing the limit and impetuous. I realized Jules disappeared when we were supposed to elope in Reno and I never saw her again."

"May I start asking questions, because I think it'll help me to better understand where you're going," Mom commented.

"Of course," I agreed.

"You're telling me all this because you didn't listen to the advice you were given and things changed. Is that right?"

Steve Wilhelm's: Another Time To Love

I nodded my head. "Yes."

"How bad?"

"Pretty bad," I said. I was searching Mom's face for any sign of disbelief, but her countenance was steadfast and trusting. "Mom, I'm actually surprised at how well you're taking everything I'm telling you."

"Daniel, trust me, it's quite a stretch, but I don't see any reason why you would go to all the trouble to make this up. But tell me about the things you have changed? Instead of being married to Lizzie, you're married to Jules. Isn't that what you both had planned anyway?"

"Yes," I said and then I told her of the other things I'd experienced since my interfering with my past

"All right, then. Let me pose another question. At some point in the other timeline, I had died, and that's why it was so good to see me again just the other day, is that right?" Mom asked.

"Yes, but you don't really want me to tell you about that, do you? It was hard enough living through losing you once before."

"Fair enough," Mom said. "So, you're going to try and go back once again to fix things? Is that going to be possible?"

"I sure hope so. I found the doctor and he believes me as well. He said he would do what he could to replicate the procedure and send me back. I've changed too many things, caused too many lives to unravel. I have to set things right. I can't bear to wake up once again and find

Steve Wilhelm's: Another Time To Love

everything has changed again. Who knows when that might happen, but it probably will."

"I remember once when I was a young girl," Mom said, "my father gave me a sealed box and told me to put it up in my closet way back on the top shelf. I asked him what it was and he told me I would find out, but not right then. Well, I did as he asked, but the longer it sat there, the more I thought about it. And the more I thought about it, the greater the need to find out what was inside."

"What happened," I asked.

"I pulled it down one Friday night when my parents were out and sat on my bed starting at the box. Finally, I couldn't take the suspense any longer and I opened it. Inside, was a note saying 'trust is a hard thing to gain. Now you have to work hard to earn it back.' I only mention this, because it seems fitting in a roundabout way. Please, don't think I'm judging you, but you were given the power to find out what you were looking for, but you weren't responsible. I can't fault you too much for that. God knows what I would have done in the same situation."

"Like, if you found yourself able to keep Dad from dying?"

"Exactly. I can't say for sure if I would do anything different from what you've done. We're human, we're full of emotions and we sometimes let those make the decisions for us, right or wrong."

"Mom, I really screwed up," I said.

Steve Wilhelm's: Another Time To Love

"You did. I agree," she had told the absolute truth. "But, you realize the mistake and want to fix it, so that makes a difference. It doesn't condone what's been done, but if you are successful, then no one will know the difference."

"Part of me doesn't want to, and I had to fight that side because you would be gone. So would Jeff for that matter."

"But I'm not sure you wouldn't know any difference, Daniel. It would be like nothing was wrong in the first place. It would be just another day in the life as it was."

"I can only hope," I said.

"When are you planning on doing all this?"

"Monday morning," I answered.

"Do me a favor, before you do," Mom asked.

"Of course," I said. "Anything."

"Just swing by, or call and say goodbye."

I stood up and went to Mom's side of the table. I leaned over and gave her a bear hug from behind. She pulled my arms tight and I could tell she didn't want to let go. I felt tears were ready to burst through the dam holding them back. "I will, Mom."

"Good," she patted me on the arms. "Now is there anything else you would like to tell me?"

"Um, well, yes. I found out this morning Maggie is pregnant."

***

Steve Wilhelm's: Another Time To Love

"And what did your mom say when you told her that?" Lizzie asked, as she browsed over her menu. I had called her last night to see what her Sunday looked like, and was pleased when she told me she had the day off from all of her jobs. It was her one day she allowed herself to rest and relax. I asked if she would mind spending the day together, have lunch and maybe take in a movie. Lizzie then suggested we take the ferry over to Bainbridge Island and spend the day there.

"What did she say? Well, she was ecstatic and quite beside herself. Then, when I mentioned that Maggie intends to abort the baby, she became visibly distraught. I think she loved the thought of having a great grandchild before she passes. She made me promise to try and persuade Maggie to change her mind."

"And... how would you feel about being a grandfather?" Lizzie tried to get out of me.

"That's a good question," I answered. I looked over my own menu. We were sitting at a table on the deck overlooking the waterfront at 'Doc's Marine Grill.' It was a beautiful sunny day, with just a slight breeze and barely a cloud in the sky. "I've been so caught up in my own issues that I haven't given it a lot of thought. I think ultimately it would be better for Maggie if she was a little older, and certainly out of school. It's always better for a child to have two parents, and I don't know how serious Maggie's relationship with the father, Andy is. I just don't think it's the right time for a baby for her. Of course, I would prefer she consider adoption over abortion, but that's just me."

Steve Wilhelm's: Another Time To Love

"Sounds like you do have some good thoughts," Lizzie commented. "But, you haven't said how you would feel being a grandfather."

"Oh, yeah. I think I would be an awesome grandfather!"

"I think you would be great at that," Lizzie said with a smile. "I already know what a great and devoted father you are." She closed her menu and set it down on the table in front of her.

We ordered our lunch and ate our delicious meals while enjoying the sights and sounds of the marina. The enticing atmosphere allowed us to enjoy our dinner in peace. After we were finished, we fancied a stroll and left the restaurant and to roam around, going into a few of the quaint gift shops and marveling at many of the local offerings. I commented on how clean the air smelled with so few cars. We did have to be wary of all the bicycle riders, as the bicycle was the favored mode of transportation on the island.

Lizzie then pointed to a sign above a shop ahead of us. 'Mora Iced Creamery' it read. "Let's go in there," she squealed like a child. I smiled as we entered. "Oh look, they make their own ice cream with local ingredients and can even ship to anywhere." I shot a quick glance over her shoulder at the brochure she was reading.

I ordered a pint of strawberry and she got a pint of green tea flavor and we sat outside in front of the store to enjoy our treats.

Steve Wilhelm's: Another Time To Love

"Daniel, this is delicious, you should definitely taste some," Lizzie said, holding out a portion to me on her spoon.

"I'll take a rain check for the moment," I said. "Not sure how the tea will taste with the strawberry, but I'll take your word for the how good it I'm sure it is."

Lizzie took the last bite of her ice cream and then set the pint down. She licked her lips jubilantly, extremely satisfied with her choice. "I had a dream last night. Would you like to know what it was about?"

"I don't know," I said. "Do I want to know?" Of course I wanted to know, I thought.

"It was a rather selfish dream, I'll start you with that."

"Oh, well I *love* selfish dreams," I admitted. "Please continue."

"It starts years back, when we were living together at school. Everything was the same, except that when we were taking care of your mom when she got sick and recovered, Jules never returned. You and I married and had a little girl of our own. She was the most beautiful baby I had ever seen. We named her Megan. Then, the dream flashed forward and years later, we were still as happy as ever. One day, I found out I was pregnant again and right after I told you, the dream ended and I woke up."

"That's so frustrating," I said. "I can say that from personal experience. Up until waking up, I think it was a really great dream. Very interesting."

Steve Wilhelm's: Another Time To Love

"I think so, too," Lizzie agreed.

"That kind of ties in to what we were talking about Thursday. You remember the 'what-if's' we were contemplating?"

"Yes, I do and I did find the life from the dream to have been wonderfully warm and happy." Lizzie looked at me. "Sure beats my current existence all to hell."

She couldn't have been more perfectly on target in that, I thought. I didn't know why she would've dreamt that now of all times. It almost mirrored the life that I gave up when I first came back. I gazed into Lizzie's eyes, trying to think of something to say. She took my hand into hers.

"Hey, I wasn't fishing for any certain thought from you," she said. "I just wanted to share something amazing that I experienced. I'm okay, so don't worry. Not going off the deep end just because of the way things are."

"I'm sorry, Lizzie," I said. "I do wish things were different. I meant what I told you when I said I never stopped loving you."

"I know, Daniel," Lizzie squeezed my hand. "I love you too. I will cherish being able to make love with you again, the heights you took me to. It was all so perfect and I don't regret one single moment of it. Not only that, but our deep connection. We're perfect for each other."

"I have no regrets either," I said, truthfully.

We tossed our empty pints and began walking slowly back to the car at the ferry dock. She put her hand on my arm and it felt comfortable.

Steve Wilhelm's: Another Time To Love

"Daniel, can I ask you something?"

"Of course," I said stopping mid-stride. "Ask me anything."

"This is purely hypothetical, so please don't read anything into it, okay?"

"Okay," I paused, now wondering what was on her mind.

"You know we didn't use anything when we made love and I was fine with that, because I know my cycle. It should have come Friday or Saturday, but it still hasn't."

"Are you saying that we might be pregnant?" I asked, my heart skipping a beat.

"No, not at all," Lizzie answered. "It's way too early to know. I just kind of wanted to know how you would be in the off-off chance that I did get pregnant. Which, I'm sure won't be anything to worry about. You came with such great force that I'm sure the travel time of your wonderful seeds was greatly enhanced, but it does take time for nature to work properly and I'm sure my period will show any day now."

"Honestly, I would be one happy, but confused man," I said. "I'd be confused only because of our situation, but happy because we may have created a child, if that makes any sense."

"Oh, Daniel," Lizzie said, and stopped to kiss me. "I couldn't be happier with what you just said."

It was the truth, but now I had things that begged for consideration. The time of the procedure was looming, and maybe it was for the best. Things were starting to

Steve Wilhelm's: Another Time To Love

spiral out of control once again. As much as I would be happy if Lizzie were pregnant, what would that mean for Jules? How would I ever explain this to her? She had us separate to give us time for self-contemplation, not going out and meeting with an ex, sleeping with her and getting pregnant! Jules didn't deserve that. She might be going through her own issues, and maybe gripe a lot, but she loves me— what have I done?

Stop it! I told myself. All of these thoughts will not solve anything. It'll just make things that much more convoluted.

***

The smell of breakfast was overwhelmingly aromatic. I got out of bed and quickly showered, shaved and made my way down the stairs and into the kitchen. My nostrils guiding me in the direction of the spread. Mom was standing over the stove turning the sausage so they finished cooking evenly. The scrambled eggs and French toast and hash browns were all ready to be served and waiting in their respective bowls in the oven.

Suddenly, I felt hands reach around my stomach and fingers tickled me. "Hey there, sleepyhead," Jules said. "I was wondering if you were ever going to come down for breakfast!"

I turned myself around in Jules' arms and looked into her beautiful smiling face. I felt my eyes watering with tears. She caressed my lips with her own. Her breath

Steve Wilhelm's: Another Time To Love

was scented with toothpaste and orange juice and in that moment I was in heaven. Her body relaxed, as if she meant to end the embrace, but I held her tight against me for a few seconds longer. She stepped back when I finally let her go. She had a quizzical look on her face.

"Oh, don't mind him, Julia," Mom said. "He's got a thing for hugs lately." The two of them laughed at me, and I felt my cheeks growing warm with embarrassment.

"Yes, don't mind me," I said, confused. What was happening? This was all too familiar and I had a vivid sense of déjà vu. "Hey, please don't wait on me to serve up. I just forgot something upstairs." I excused myself and went back to my bedroom.

I looked at myself in the mirror above my dresser. My face looked haggard and old, almost scary. What was going on? Goosebumps were rising on my arms and the hairs on the back of my neck were beginning to stand at attention.

"Daniel, are you okay?" I heard my mom's voice from downstairs. "Come on down and eat while there's still food!"

She had a point. Jules had a way of packing food down and never showing a bit of weight. Her metabolism was out of this world. I collected myself and went back down to the kitchen. There was so much food waiting, it seemed way too much for three people.

"Jeez, Mom. Did you invite the whole neighborhood, or what?" I said.

Steve Wilhelm's: Another Time To Love

"Well, you know how I am with my breakfasts, and knowing how much you eat, I wanted to make sure there was plenty for Julia," Mom said.

"Mom, you're embarrassing me," I said. This conversation was way too familiar. I knew I had to do something, but I wasn't quite sure what it was. I began to pile the food onto my plate and then stopped when I realized how rude it was not to let Jules fill her plate first.

We all dug into the food on our plates and finally when we were finished, Mom got up and started to clear the table. I looked at Jules and smiled. "You look very nice this morning," I said.

"Why thank you, Danny," she smiled back, her face beaming with adoration.

"I think it's best if we break up, Jules," I said, the words coming out of nowhere. I had not known that was what I was going to say.

Jules face went from bright and cheerful to clouded and confused. "What? Why?"

Mom turned off the water in the sink and the room became eerily quiet. "Daniel Allen," she said. "What's gotten into you?"

Jules stood up and came over to me. "Sweetie, what's wrong? Are you not feeling well?"

I stood as well, facing Jules. "I'm fine. It's just not working out. It's for the best." I said, there was no emotion in my voice.

"I don't understand," she cried, her eyes clouding with tears. "You don't mean it. I know you!"

Steve Wilhelm's: Another Time To Love

"It's been fun, but life goes on," I said.

Jules stared at me, and I saw a look of anger in her eyes. "I hate you, Danny," she said and before I knew it, her arm moved like a lightning bolt and I felt the sting of the slap on my cheek before I heard the sound of it.

***

My eyes snapped open and I sat up in the bed, my body shivered as it was covered in sweat. Where was I? I reached over and pulled the cord to turn on the bedside lamp. I was in Jeff's guestroom. I wiped my forehead and slid back down and rested my head into the pillow, breathing out a huge gasp of relief. It was a dream. Uncannily realistic, but thank God just a dream. I shook my head slightly, hoping I didn't have the beginnings of a pounding headache, but there was nothing. I turned off the lamp and laid back, staring at the window across the room. I could see the moon shining brightly through the curtains, coaxing me to go back to sleep.

Was the dream a sign of things to come? Is that where I need to tell Mathew to steer me when we begin the procedure? Something about the scenario didn't feel right. If I were to actually handle things that way, break up with Jules out of the blue like that, couldn't it set off a new chain of events that might cause more disasters in the future? What if Jules' anger caused her to do something that we would regret? I must remember to ask Mathew about that.

Steve Wilhelm's: Another Time To Love

I thought about it for a few minutes more. And it occurred to me, that maybe the best way for me to stop myself from going back in the first place would be to somehow make sure the card from Jules never falls out of that yearbook in the first place. Or, better yet, somehow remove that particular box from the equation and then I never would think about Jules. How would I do that? As far as I knew, the procedure only sends consciousness back to the past in the younger body. I couldn't remove the box without knowing why, and then that would defeat the purpose of trying to make sure I didn't think about Jules. It was so damn confusing, I thought.

This whole weekend for the most part, was pretty good. I got to spend some quality time with those I very much cared for and said goodbye to the ones I won't see again if things work out the way I hoped they would. Meeting up with Lizzie again was what had helped me solidify my decision to go through with seeing Mathew and having him attempt to send me back.

I hadn't planned on the being intimate with her, but I'm glad I was. And even now knowing there could be a new life created from not using protection, it makes me miss what she and I had. In the original timeline, there wasn't a new baby on the way, but in the altered reality, there was. Either way, I just want to be back in Lizzie's arms and living the life I was taking for granted. I will never do that again.

Then, Maggie's pregnancy popped into my mind. What am I supposed to do with that information? I

Steve Wilhelm's: Another Time To Love

handled things pretty well when Jules and I had our talk with her, and as much as I would not want her to go through with the abortion tomorrow, in the long run, is it going to matter? Of course it will, to her and the baby, but in this reality. Not the one I'm trying to get back to. And then there's that possibility that Lizzie might be pregnant, I thought. Perhaps, I should reconsider and postpone the procedure for a couple of weeks. Give myself time to work with Maggie and see what I could do to convince her to keep the baby. It would also give time to see if Lizzie is positive, or not. Or, I could just go ahead with the plan and nothing else would matter.

Or, (and I'm throwing around quite of few of them) what if I were to wake up and find myself in another reality that is totally different from this one and the last one? No, I thought to myself determined. I had to stick with the program. There was no turning back now. I sat up once again and fluffed up the pillows and straightened out the covers. I needed to get some good sleep so I could wake up and be as refreshed as I could and not look back.

Steve Wilhelm's: Another Time To Love

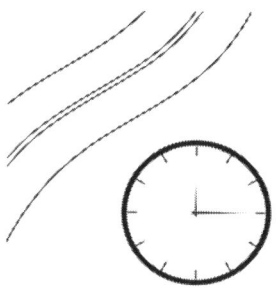

Chapter Nine

The morning was cold and wet. The roaring clouds were dark with pent up moisture and threatened to unload a deluge of watery rage. It looked like it might precipitate all day. However the weather, I was in a good mood. I'd been able to finally get back to sleep and seemed to stay that way until the alarm went off four hours later. Jeff was off to work by the time I was up, showered and ready to go. He and I had said what we needed to after I had returned from the day with Lizzie. He wished me luck and hoped he never saw me again but I understood what he meant.

    My good spirits hadn't dampened even after my phone call to work and talking with my boss. To be fair, I probably should have talked to him Friday, but I hadn't thought things through entirely. I did tell him I was much better, but that I needed one more day, because I had an important appointment with the doctor, which was true.

Steve Wilhelm's: Another Time To Love

He told me it was okay, but if I wasn't at work first thing in the morning with a new attitude and a clear head, I shouldn't worry about showing up at all.

Now, I was braving some of the worst traffic on I-405 than I can recall seeing in a long time. I was not stressing, however. I had given myself plenty of time to get to Mathew's office. If my scheduling was correct, I should have a good hour to kill before it was time. I parked in the parking garage near Mathew's office and made my way down to the street. As I stepped onto the sidewalk, I almost collided with a woman walking with her head down and holding her purse above her. Not the best way to keep the rain off, I thought. In a pinch, I suppose anything was worth trying.

She stopped and looked up. "Excuse me, sir," she began and then we recognized each other. "Daddy? What are you doing here?"

"I'm . . . uh . . . well, I have a doctor's appointment." I stammered.

"Sure, Daddy," Maggie said. She looked at me, scrutinizing my face. "You're here because you want to talk me out of the abortion, aren't you?"

"Oh, that's right, that's today, same time as my appointment," I remembered. "No, seriously, that's not why I'm here."

"It's all right," Maggie said. "If it makes any difference, I'm not going through with it. I'm going to see them and cancel, but see if I can get some information on adoption procedures."

Steve Wilhelm's: Another Time To Love

"You are?" I asked, frankly surprised. "I'm proud of you sweetheart, truly I am. I believe in pro-choice, but I also want what's best for you."

"I know that, Daddy," she said with a smile. "I've always known that."

"Hey, let's get out of the rain and grab a quick coffee before our appointments, shall we?" I suggested.

"I would like that," Maggie answered.

A block away, Maggie pointed out a little diner that looked like it might have the perfect father-daughter atmosphere. We went inside and found a quiet booth in a corner. The waitress brought us both a cup of coffee and asked if we needed menus. I told her just the coffee for now and she left for another table.

"How is your mother doing?" I asked.

"She's fine, but you know that," Maggie smiled. "Remember the intervention?"

"Yes, dear," I smiled. "I remember your mother putting that together herself. You also know she can sometimes put on a very good show."

"I know," Maggie agreed. "She's okay, more or less. She really misses you Daddy. She told me she really doesn't know if she did something or what, but I know she isn't going to give up on you guys."

"She shouldn't."

"So things are going to get better? Really?" Maggie asked, almost pleading that I would respond positively.

"I'm doing what I can to make the best changes, Mags. Trust me on that."

Steve Wilhelm's: Another Time To Love

"I know Mom can be a real bitch sometimes," Maggie said.

I raised my eyebrows in surprise. Had I just been sipping my coffee, it would have been all over Maggie at her statement. "Maggie, this is your mother we're talking about, have some respect."

"I am. There was another word I could have used. I'm not sure you would have approved of that one."

"I'm not sure I approve of the 'b' word, either," I said. "But yes, she can be. I can be a real bastard at times, as well. It wasn't that at all. I love her, very, very much."

"Can you tell me what then? I'm not and I won't be judgmental Daddy. I just really care and want the best for you."

"I really don't know how to explain everything, Mags. I certainly won't pretend to understand much of what's been happening either."

"Is it anything I did? I know my grades haven't been what they should be, but I promise I'll work harder and do better." Maggie was so cute trying to take the weight of my problems on her shoulders.

"Oh, sweetie, I love you to death, you know that?" I smiled and put my hand on hers. "Listen. You have done nothing but good. You are a true inspiration and any parent out there would hard-pressed to have raised a daughter as special as you."

"Thank you, Daddy," Maggie said. She squeezed my hand and then took it to wipe a tear that had made spilled onto her cheek. "I'm sorry for all the questions. Most of

Steve Wilhelm's: Another Time To Love

my friends don't have parents who are still together and I've always bragged about you guys. I just want to be able to keep bragging."

"I know, I want you to as well," I said. I added some creamer to my coffee, stirred and took a sip. "Can I ask you something now?"

"Sure," Maggie said.

"This guy you've been seeing, his name is Alan, right?"

"Yeah, that's right," Maggie looked at me. "He's really a good guy."

"I figured that. I don't think you'd pick anyone who wasn't. Were you able to talk to him about your pregnancy?"

"Actually, yes," Maggie told me. "I called him right before you left Saturday and then he came over and we talked. You should have seen him, Daddy. His face got all white and I thought he was seriously going to pass out. If it wasn't so serious a conversation, I would have started laughing. I felt bad enough trying to keep a serious face. That smile wanted out so bad."

"Maggie, you're bad," I smiled.

"Just saying," Maggie smiled. "Anyway, Alan was very understanding and asked if I wanted to keep it. He said he would marry me if I did, that he would be there every step of the way."

"Did he mean it or did he think I would pull out the shotgun if he didn't say that?"

Steve Wilhelm's: Another Time To Love

"Now who's being bad?" Maggie laughed. lightly "No, I knew he meant it. I told him I was going to take care of it and if he wanted to help, that would be fine. I thought he was going to cry. You know what he said?"

"What did he say?" I asked.

"He looked at me and told me that would be a really selfish thing to do. He said there are probably many, many couples out there who have tried to have children, but can't. He said that it would be the right thing to do instead of having an abortion, give someone the chance to have a child. He was so sweet, but he's also right." You could see the lasting impression of Alan's decision embedded in her eyes.

"You never cease to amaze me, my wonderful child." I revealed, she had truly impressed me with her wisdom.

"I'm not a child anymore, Daddy," she reminded me.

"I know that, but in my mind's eye, you'll always be my little girl," I replied. "That's my prerogative. You'll understand that yourself one day."

"I love you too," Maggie expressed.

My heart was so full of love and affection, if it busted and I died right then and there, I'd die happy.

"What are you seeing the doctor for?" Maggie inquired. Panic spread like wild-fire through my nerves.

"It's nothing serious, just a checkup, is all. It's nothing to worry about." I couldn't tell her what I was doing, of course. Even if I felt comfortable in doing it,

Steve Wilhelm's: Another Time To Love

Maggie had enough to worry about, and I didn't want anything getting back to Jules. God knows she didn't need the complications that would stem from the burden of carrying this knowledge. I doubt either of them would believe any of it anyway.

"Okay, good to hear." Maggie said. "I'm glad things are working out. I'm really looking forward to having you and mom back together, again. The world just isn't right otherwise, and it stopped the day you left the house."

If only she knew, I thought ironically. "Thanks for spending time with your old man. I can't tell you what a pleasure it always is." I flashed her a toothy grin and scratched at the bottom of my chin just thinking about what the future would be like after the procedure.

"Daddy, don't be silly. I'm always going to be here for you," Maggie laughed. "I'll call you later, okay? I'll fill you in on everything I found out."

"I love you, Maggie," I verbalized, getting up. I went over to her side of the booth and helped her up. We hugged and I gave her a kiss on the cheek.

"Love you too, Daddy."

We walked out of the diner and hugged each other once more, and then I watched as she turned strolled down the sidewalk to her vehicle. It had stopped raining and the sun was trying to force its way through the cumbrous clouds. I made it back to Mathew's building with ten minutes to spare. Now, I wondered how smart it was to have caffeine before we began the procedure. I

Steve Wilhelm's: Another Time To Love

shook my head as I walked inside and pressed the button for the elevator. The receptionist was not at her desk when I made finally made it, but as soon as the door had closed, the doctor came in from another room. "I gave Nicole the day off so there would be no distractions while we're working," he told me after we shook hands. "I'm glad you didn't change your mind about today. I think it will be good for both of us." He had a sense of giddiness about him that wasn't present the last time I visited this office.

"I just want everything to go back to the way it was, before I was stupid and played as if I could mimic God," I admitted, completely sorry for my stubbornness. "I've made peace with everything, and saw the people I wanted to see before I do this, especially my mom and my best friend. Both of them had died in the original reality and it was great catching up. By the way, I wasn't thinking and had some coffee with my daughter just before coming here. Will that be a hindrance to our endeavor?"

"I believe it shouldn't make too much of an impact," Mathew answered. "I mean, as long as it wasn't more than three cups."

"No, it was just one cup," I commented.

He took me into a familiar looking back room. Familiar, in that it looked just like I remembered the first time I visited this place. There was a hospital bed and a shelved metal cart next to it that had housed a monitor and other various medical machines. Behind the bed, there was a window that would probably allow Mathew to view the proceedings from a separate room, just like the first time. Even though it was an anxious setting, it put my mind at ease. I was finally getting everything I ever wanted back. I just never knew what I was missing.

Mathew went into the back room and returned with a hospital gown for me to wear. "Here, If you would remove your shirt and put this on, please. That would be the only thing I request before I begin to hook you up." I did as he requested and then Mathew instructed me to lie back on the uncomfortable bed he had provided for the procedure. He began to hook up electrodes to various parts of my chest and arms, and placed a headband on my head with wires that attached to the machines on the cart.

"Are you still using that serum with the mild narcotic to help me relax?" I asked hoping beyond measure that he was. I was more than nervous, I was petrified about what the future would look like this time.

"I don't know the exact composition of the solution we used before, but this serum should be the same, or a better formula. Either way, it will cause you no lasting discomfort," Mathew said as he pulled a syringe out of his lab coat pocket. "Once I inject you with the solution, I want you to clear your mind of everything except where you wish to go. Have you considered the destination?"

"Well, I think. It might be best to go to the point when I first discovered I couldn't remember what had happened to Jules. I want to somehow stop myself from deciding to find out what happened. Basically, I need to

Steve Wilhelm's: Another Time To Love

prevent myself from meeting you, Mathew. No offense, I mean you're a cool guy, but you know what I mean."

"Of course," Mathew said, nodding his head. "I take no offense at that. I don't believe it will make a difference to my research, as I'm sure there would be other opportunities to further it if you had not been there to be a subject."

"What do you think will happen to me here, providing things work as I hope?" I asked him curiously.

"I think that the Daniel that wakes up here on the bed will be the Daniel that he was before you entered into his body and brain. I honestly don't know that for sure, since we don't really have any data to base that on. That's an excellent question, however."

"Well, I suppose there's no time like the present to get the ball rolling," I quoted.

He moved over to the cart and turned on the monitor, flipping a few switches on the other machines. I heard a slight whirring noise as they powered up and some beeps and clicks as I saw the screen begin to show my heart beat and other vital signs. Mathew smiled and turned to look at me. "I believe we are ready to begin. Ready?"

"Shoot me up," I encouraged.

He took the cap off the needle and positioned it on my forearm. I felt the needle break the skin and the sensation of warmth spread through my body as the fluid was injected into my bloodstream. As I remembered from before, in a few minutes, I felt content and serene. It was

Steve Wilhelm's: Another Time To Love

as if I didn't have a care in the world. If worse came to worse, and nothing happened, I needed to talk to him about marketing his serum as a stress reliever. I would bet money that it could be a very profitable venture.

    I closed my eyes and thought about the afternoon I had been in the basement on that day, sifting through boxes for photos. I remembered it had been hot and muggy sort of day, and I wished I had brought more than one cold beer down there with me. I could see the motes of dust floating in the air, and felt the beads of sweat accumulating on my forehead. I remembered how my shirt was sticking to my back and how a cold shower would be so amazing after I was finished. I heard soft music from somewhere in the background that methodically hummed as I worked. I wasn't sure what the music was, or exactly where it was coming from. Then there was darkness.

    I opened my eyes slowly and realized I was sitting in the basement on a stool amid stacks of mostly unlabeled boxes. Hmmm, I thought. This was a good sign. The procedure seems to have taken me back to the day of the original 'crime' as it were. I felt myself reaching for the box on the floor in front of me. That's the box, I thought. The one with the letterman's jacket, yearbook and cards. That's the box I don't want to open, but for some reason, I seem to keep reaching for it. The box that would forever change my past, present and future. Such a funny thing, to be so intimidated by something so small. My fingers

Steve Wilhelm's: Another Time To Love

touched the rough edges of the cardboard. "NO!" I called out, but no voice came from my throat, yet my hands stopped as I had requested.

"What the fuck?" I heard myself say aloud, but curiously, I hadn't initiated that phrase.

"Do not open that box," I thought.

"Who's that," my voice came out. My head turned from side to side, looking around the garage. This was peculiar.

"I'm you," I articulated. This was not going to work. It appeared that my old self had control of the body and I was merely the fly on the wall. This is what Mathew had been attempting the first time around. Damn it! Of course, it had to start working now of all times, I thought. I needed to gain control over my body, to take charge of all my thoughts and everything I did.

I remembered a movie I'd seen where there were two minds trying to control one body and what one of them did to take over. I know the movie was fiction, but what the hell, what would it hurt for me to try? I held my breath and pushed hard, almost like I was trying to clear the air out of my clogged ears, or trying to hold in the expanding smoke of a hit of weed from a bong. Suddenly, I heard and felt a loud pop and my head cleared. It was the same feeling I got after a good sneeze. Clarity.

I stood, trying to move my hand to touch the stool and surprisingly, it did. I tried to do some jumping jacks and it worked with no resistance. I recited the alphabet forward and backward, I smiling as I completed the task.

Steve Wilhelm's: Another Time To Love

Whatever I had done to put my other mind to rest and take control, it worked. I had actually gained mastery over my own body, but for how long? The other thought was, what do I do now? I needed some air, it was too hot in the basement. I reached for the beer that I had and wasn't too surprised to find it warm. Now, I needed air *and* a fresh, cold beer.

    I went into the kitchen and opened the refrigerator. The cool air from inside hit my face and it felt exquisite. I grabbed a cold beer from the box on the lower shelf and walked into the living room as I twisted the cap off. Everything looked normal, or as I remembered, which was another good sign. I saw the portrait we had made two years prior hanging on the wall above the fireplace mantel. Myself, Lizzie and Maggie. No, not Maggie. It would be Megan if everything was back to normal. I took the beer out to the patio and sat down. I pulled out my cell phone and scrolled through the contacts. There was Lizzie and two names down was Megan. I breathed a sigh of relief. Out of habit, I swiped on Lizzie's name and put the phone to my ear, hearing the ringer I waited.

    "Hello sweetheart," she answered.

    "Hi Babe," I responded in return, comforted by her voice.

    "What's going on? Is everything okay?" She asked.

    "Nothing's wrong," I said. "I just wanted to hear your voice and tell you how much I love you."

    "Daniel, that's . . . well, I just wasn't expecting that at all," Lizzie replied. "I love you, too."

Steve Wilhelm's: Another Time To Love

"How is everything out there in the east?" I asked. "Is Megan treating you all right? She hasn't ditched you for her friends, or anything rude like that, has she?"

"No," Lizzie laughed. "She hasn't. At least not so far, anyway. I haven't done anything to embarrass her much yet, so we'll give her a little more time. Other than that, things are good. The university is so beautiful and for the most part, all the kids have been very nice and respectful."

"That's good to hear. Does it make you miss the good old days?"

"Not a chance in the world," Lizzie answered. "I'm quite content with our life and especially you, my most thoughtful husband and lover."

"Keep that up and I'll be on the first plane out there," I cautioned with a smile.

"You know I would love that," Lizzie said. "I'd book us a nice room at the University Inn & Suites here. Honestly, I wouldn't mind a good upgrade from the room I'm staying in right now."

"Why, what's wrong with it?"

"Oh, it's really okay. The only real bad thing is you are not here to share the bed with me."

"I miss you so very much, Lizzie. When you come home, I think we should go somewhere together, you know, like a special vacation. Someplace we haven't been before."

"What's gotten into you, Daniel?" Lizzie asked. "We haven't gone away like that for a while. And I'm certainly

Steve Wilhelm's: Another Time To Love

not complaining. Anytime we're together is special. What made you think about this now?

"I don't know. Maybe just random thoughts," I said. "But wouldn't you think it's a good idea? We should be spontaneous and celebrate our life together any chance we can. You never know when things could change and we can't anymore. I want the best for you, for us. Never ever take anything for granted."

"You are incorrigible, Daniel," Lizzie said. "And I can't tell you how much I love you for that! Of course I'd like to go somewhere with you. Plan something out and surprise me when I get back."

"I'm on it," I said.

"Sweetie, I've got to go," Lizzie said. "I'm supposed to meet Megan for a tour of something or another, I don't remember." Lizzie laughed.

"Give her a hug and a kiss for me. Tell her I love her."

"I will Babe. Thank you so much for the call, you totally made my day," Lizzie said.

"Bye for now," I said.

"Bye for now," Lizzie repeated.

I heard a click and then there was silence on the line, but my heart was singing. I finished my beer and went inside to put the bottle in the recycle bin. I grabbed my jacket and keys and headed to the car. A drive sounded good, I thought, smiling. I drove around aimlessly for an hour before deciding to head back towards home. It wasn't a conscious decision that led me to where I

Steve Wilhelm's: Another Time To Love

ended up. It was more like I was on autopilot and wasn't thinking. I found myself turning into the parking lot of the tavern near the house. That's okay, I thought. A whiskey and Coke does in fact sound good right now. I parked my car and went inside.

I sat at the counter at the end of the bar away from the door. There were only a handful of people I could see in the place, plus the bartender. A couple was playing pool and three were engaged at the dartboard. One of the guys suddenly jumped up and down and shouted, "Hat trick, hat trick!!" I wondered what he was talking about, because I didn't see any kind of a hat on his head.

"What'll you have?" the bartender asked, after I had made myself comfortable.

"Whiskey and Coke, and make it a double if you would," I ordered.

"Sure thing. Any particular brand?"

"The one closest . . . no, check that," I said, remembering what I had said before. "How about we make bartender's choice." Then I leaned in closer to him. "Hey, dumb question, I know, but what the hell is a 'hat trick?'" I whispered.

"Nah, it's cool. If you're not into darts, I can understand you not knowing," he said, leaning in. "It's when you throw all three of your darts in a turn and they all land in the bull's eye." He whispered back.

"Ah, okay, that makes sense, probably a high scoring throw. That would make sense because that guy got all excited and started jumping up and down."

Steve Wilhelm's: Another Time To Love

"Ya think?" the bartender laughed good-naturedly a little and made my drink without much to say.

The first drink was quite satisfying and I ordered a second to follow. I sipped at it and stared at the television on the wall up above the bar. I tried to get interested in the soccer game that was being featured, but my mind wandered to thoughts of Lizzie. Where would be a good place to take her on a romantic get-away, I wondered. Maybe Scotland or Ireland? I know she and I have talked about those places before, and added them to our list of places to visit before we died. Either destination would be more than fine with me. I made a mental note to start checking into things when I got home. The thought of Lizzie's reaction to my ideas, her bright smiling face pleased me to no end.

For the first time in a long time, I felt things were finally coming around. I could let go of the thought that I hoped to see the light at the end of the tunnel and replace it with 'there's the light!' It seemed to me, that if I completely avoided ever seeing or running into Mathew, I would not be sent back and everything would be set to the way it was supposed to be, to the way it was before. Closing my eyes, I lifted my drink upward and silently toasted to whatever greater power there was for allowing me a new beginning.

"My friend, I wish you could spread some of that good cheer you must be feeling over my way," said a voice from next to me.

Steve Wilhelm's: Another Time To Love

"Excuse me?" I turned and was surprised to see Mathew. It had escaped me that I was at the tavern where I'd first met him. I almost acknowledged him by name and then caught myself. I didn't want to do, or say anything to get myself off the track of setting things to normal. But having thought that, I didn't want to be rude and ignore the man. "I sure wish I could," I said.

Mathew looked at me curiously. "Have we met previously?"

"I've been told I have a familiar face," I answered. I looked Mathew over as nonchalant as I could. He looked the same as that day I first met him. His brown hair was unkempt and his glasses were slightly smudged and sat crookedly on his nose. He had a two day old growth on his face and his eyes were bloodshot. He looked as if he hadn't slept in days.

"Well, I'm sorry," he said. "Forgive me if I've disturbed you. He picked up his drink and drained it down in a quick swallow and gestured to the bartender for a refill.

"No, you're fine. You're not disturbing me at all," I said. "Are you okay? I'm not at all trying to come across as rude, but you look as if you've seen better days."

"I've seen better, yes. I've definitely had better days, better months, even, you know," he said, then stuck his hand out. "Mathew, Mathew Stevens."

I shook his hand. "My name's Daniel," I said. "It's nice to meet you." I had the urge to wipe my hand off

Steve Wilhelm's: Another Time To Love

when we released from the shake, fo his hand was extremely clammy.

"What are you drinking, Daniel," Mathew asked and then signaled to the bartender before I could answer. "Get my friend here another of what he's drinking."

"No, that's okay," I said. "I mean, I appreciate it, but you really don't have to." I've been drinking doubles and on an empty stomach which could lead to bad judgement, I thought.

"Nonsense, I've been here for a couple of hours and you're the first person to have given me the time of day. Except for the bartender, but he's paid to be cordial. It's the least I can offer," Mathew told me.

"Well, I will say thank you, then." I finished my drink so I didn't have to look like a two-fisted drinker. I thanked the bartender when he served me my fresh cocktail. "Thank you again, Mathew," I started to rise from my stool.

"Some people are less sociable than others, I've noted," Mathew spoke, staring at me. "They just come to bars to drink their troubles away."

"Yes, I've been there," I revealed.

"I must admit that's what I'm doing here now," Mathew said.

I know that, Mathew, I thought. "I'm sorry," I said. I was going to do my best to extricate myself from this conversation without being impolite.

"My partner, who I work with – I mean, worked with, was involved in a horrific automobile accident. He

Steve Wilhelm's: Another Time To Love

was hit by a drunk driver and badly injured. They just took him off of life support."

Please someone call my cell phone, I thought. Any reason to leave would be greatly appreciated. "That's horrible," I said. "I'm so very sorry."

"I'm a psychotherapist and researcher. He and I were working on a theoretical procedure for aiding those with memory problems to find solutions. It really was a two person project, but unfortunately I must now take over it all myself." Mathew took a large swallow of his drink and wiped his lips. "We were on the verge of a breakthrough." He stopped and looked embarrassed.

"That's good, isn't it?" I asked.

"I'm sorry," he said.

"What's wrong?"

"I seem to be less . . . well more distraught over our project being hampered than by his death. That doesn't seem right."

"Maybe you just need some time to sort things out," I ventured. "You know, try and put things in the right perspective."

Mathew looked as if he was pondering my advice for a moment. "Yes, maybe so . . . maybe so. That sounds exactly what I might have told any of my patients at one time or another. Bravo, my friend. Thank you. You've given me some very encouraging words. Might I return the favor sometime?"

"Of course, I don't see why not," I said. Now was no time better than any to try and excuse myself. "I really have to go make an important phone call. Why don't you give me your card if you have one and I'll be in touch."

"That would be fine," Mathew said and reached into his coat and fished out a card. He handed it to me. "Thank you for putting up with my rantings, I know it's probably not an everyday occurrence you have to go through."

I stood, "No, it's not," I agreed. "But, it's been a pleasure to meet you. Perhaps we'll meet again. Thank you again for the drink." I pulled out my cell phone and started to walk away.

"Yes, perhaps we will," I heard Mathew say as I gave the bartender a twenty dollar bill for my first two drinks. "Good to meet you Daniel."

I turned and walked towards the door. Once outside, I breathed out a sigh of relief. I got away with it.

The drive home thankfully was uneventful. I don't normally drive after drinking and I was buzzed, but I drove extra careful and made it home okay. I spent the rest of the afternoon culling through all the rest of the boxes in the garage and finally had all the photos I needed to finish the CD photo album I was surprising Lizzie with. Funny, it seemed as if it had taken a lifetime to almost finish this project.

That night, as I was in bed and doing my best to fall asleep, my mind had other ideas. It kept thinking about what might be happening to the me that was left in Mathew's office in the other reality, since I had not

Steve Wilhelm's: Another Time To Love

returned. Had I woken up and then went about my life as normal? Did I have any clue as to what I might have been doing? Did I know why I was there? Big question was, did I even wake up at all? I grabbed the remote off the nightstand and turned the television on. I needed to distract myself from all of the useless thinking if I could. The channel that came on was showing a movie that I had seen many times before. Ironically it had to do with travelling back in time. I laughed and thought how coincidental this all was. I flipped through the channels and finally settled on an old rerun of 'Gilligan's Island,' and muted the volume so I didn't have to hear it. I got comfortable under the covers and promptly fell asleep.

***

I awoke to the sound of my cell phone ringing. It was light outside and as I struggled to open my eyes, the glare of the sun through the curtains momentarily blinded me. What the hell time was it, I wondered. I didn't like to oversleep on days off. That always felt like a waste of good time. I managed to find the cell on the nightstand and brought it close to my eyes, looking at the caller ID. It said Megan.

"Hi Honey," I said groggily. "How're things going?" I heard crying on the other end and I was instantly alert. "Honey? What's wrong?" Sniffles. "Are you alright? Are you hurt? Where's Mom? Talk to me, Megan."

Steve Wilhelm's: Another Time To Love

"I . . . I'm, okay," Megan managed between sobs. "Mom is . . . she was . . . in an accident . . ."

"What?" My heart skipped a beat and I felt a chill come over me.

"She . . . left, sooner than she planned . . . she said she . . . wanted to surprise you . . . oh Daddy!" There was loud crying, sobbing.

"Take your time, baby," I said. "Deep breaths . . . tell me what happened, please?"

There was hesitation, and I heard the crying subside just a bit. "The taxi Mom was taking to the airport was . . . broadsided by a bus and . . . and it was sent into the opposite traffic and . . . then they were hit head on." Megan was crying harder now. "Mom's dead, Daddy, Mommy's gone."

My cell phone slipped from my fingers and hit the floor. I reached up and covered my eyes with my hands and screamed silently, not believing what Megan had just told me. It can't be true, I thought. I just spoke to her yesterday and . . . Megan wouldn't make something like that up. Not the way she was reacting as she told me. I felt the bedroom walls closing in on me. I was gasping and choking for air. I had to get out. I reached down and picked up my phone and managed to go outside into the middle of the backyard. I gulped the fresh air in and let the breeze blow over my hot face. Then I realized I was talking to Megan.

"Megan? Are you still there? I'm sorry, about that, I kind of lost it there," I said. She wasn't answering. I

Steve Wilhelm's: Another Time To Love

repeated hello several more times and still silence. I didn't know if we'd been disconnected, or perhaps she'd hung up. I tried calling her back several times, and it kept going right to her voicemail. I wanted to throw the cell and smash it into pieces. Over the next few hours, I was on the phone several times with the New York Police and could barely understand what they were trying to tell me. I did acknowledge when they told me how sorry they were about Lizzie. I nodded absently. They told me there had not been any criminal charges filed against anyone. The initial investigation had labeled it as a freak accident. Like that helps me or Lizzie, I thought. Even if someone had been negligent and was the cause of the accident and they were arrested, jailed and executed, that would not bring Lizzie back. I was numb to everything. They said the taxi driver had been killed along with the occupants of the vehicle that had hit the taxi head-on. I was then informed, that I would be contacted as to what I wanted to do with Lizzie's body. At that, I said I had to go and ended the call. Lizzie's body. Lizzie's body. That just sounded so final and impersonal. I sat down on the floor of the kitchen and the tears came crashing down like a sudden rain storm from swollen clouds. I leaned over and pounded my fists into the floor several times. It caused pain, but I didn't care, whatsoever. Let there be pain, it would remind me that this was all my fault. At least that was something coherent I could comprehend. I couldn't have cared less if someone had come in to the house and saw me like this. I curled up into the fetal position and cried myself to sleep.

Steve Wilhelm's: Another Time To Love

"Daniel, why did you do this to me?"
  "Daniel, I don't understand what you've done."
  "Daniel, I'm in so much pain!"
  "Where am I, Daniel?"
  "Daniel?"
  "Daniel?"

Fleeting faces, hollow voices, darkness. Cold. The voices and faces were familiar, yet not. They could be people I knew and loved, I couldn't say for sure, but I was certain they were there because of me. Because of what I'd done. How long would they haunt me? How long would I need to suffer the torment before I could finally be released, as I so desperately sought? What did I have to do to atone for my discretions? I've tried and tried to make things right, but each time I've managed to make things worse.

"You're selfish, only thinking of yourself, Daniel." The face that went with the voice was unmistakably Jeff, of that I was convinced.

"I'm so sorry, my friend," I said out loud.

"I don't believe you."

New voice. "You left me, found me, left me, I came back and now I'm dead. Was this your plan all along?" Lizzie, was it her?

"No! That's not true," I yelled. "I love you!"

"Nice way to show it." The voice trailed off.

Steve Wilhelm's: Another Time To Love

New voice. "We were soulmates, Danny." There was no denying it was Jules. "I gave you a daughter. I gave you love. Why have you left us?"

"I— ." There was no viable response that I could possibly come up with. No words that would even come close to answering that question. "I'm sorry, I never meant for any of this to happen!"

Another voice enters, this one stings beyond words. "I'm so very disappointed in you, son. I expected so much more from you." Mom.

That was too much to handle and I screamed. I woke up to find myself still on the kitchen floor. Fresh tears were coating my cheeks. I sat up and leaned back against the refrigerator door, the cold surface permeating my shirt. Feelings of guilt and shame coursed through my body. I was alone, no one to talk to, other than the angry voices in my head. Mom and Jeff were gone. There was only Megan. I had tried many, many times to return her call, but she wasn't answering. Did she too, blame me for everything? Lizzie had cut her time with Megan in New York short to come back to me. She had every right to put responsibility for Lizzie's death on me. I looked around the kitchen in despair. I was at a total loss of direction. What was I to do? There was nothing left for me here.

"But what about me, Daddy?" Megan's voice. "Are you going to leave me, too?"

"No, honey," I said, my voice sounding eerie in the quiet kitchen. "You saved me once when I gave up. I won't do that to you again." Was it Megan or Maggie who saved

Steve Wilhelm's: Another Time To Love

me when I had taken those sleeping pills and drank too much alcohol? I didn't suppose it mattered anyway. They both are the same person, aren't they? I wondered. This was all too much for my weary brain to process. I got up and knew I had to go see Mathew. I looked in my wallet and prayed his card was there. It was.

I called the number and anxiously waited for an answer. Then, I heard a click and: "Mathew Stevens."

"Mathew," I began, trying not to sound panicked. "I'm Daniel Allen. I met you at the tavern yesterday afternoon."

"Oh, yes. I remember you," Mathew said. "I'm not surprised you called."

"You aren't?" I asked.

"No, but I can't enlighten you as to why I said that."

"I need to see you if I could. As soon as possible."

"I had a notion you would. And again, I can't explain the reason. I'll clear my afternoon for you, Daniel. How soon can you be here?"

Less than a half hour later and without needing my GPS to get there, since his office was at the same spot, I had arrived. I relayed my tale to Mathew and when I had finished, he took a few minutes to process my information.

"How many different versions of me have you met?" Mathew asked.

"So you believe me then," I shook my head. "God knows I'm not convinced even I would have."

Steve Wilhelm's: Another Time To Love

"As fantastic as everything you've told me sounds, I do believe you. And it gives me great optimism for the success of the treatment program my partner and I had been working on."

"That's good news for me as well," I said. "But to answer your question, I'll say Mathew Prime, the one who originally sent me back was the first. You may very well be Mathew Prime, unless something I've done has caused this timeline to be corrupted. Then, there's Mathew Two, who sent me to this reality. But, if you are different, you would conceivably be Mathew Three. So two, possibly three Mathews I have met."

"Extremely fascinating," Mathew commented. "Tell me, have you felt any abnormal side effects due to your multiple 'travels' if you will? I mean besides the obvious alterations in the different realities?"

"Not really, though I do seem to get frequent headaches, sometimes very intense. I never used to have those."

"Interesting," Mathew noted. "It might be that the human brain is not meant to easily process the stress of 'travelling' as many times as you have. My thought would be that with the undue trauma it goes through each time, there may be damage caused to the cells. I would not be able to corroborate that without studying the wave cycles during a trip. I'm not sure I would advise you going through with another without more study."

"I'm not saying I don't believe you, Mathew," I said. "In fact, what you just told me scares the hell outta me,

Steve Wilhelm's: Another Time To Love

but honestly, it's a risk I am willing to take. I can't stay here. I have nothing. At least if I can get back to the previous timeline, everyone is there and my biggest task would be to get a large grinder and smooth over all the jagged edges."

"I can appreciate your predicament," Mathew said. "I really mean that. In fact, I was just thinking while listening to your story, what if I myself could go back and attempt to prevent my partner from being in that car accident."

"Exactly," I agreed. "What if you could?"

"From hearing what you've experienced, I don't know I'd want to actually do it. There seems to be too many unexplained variables. Too much risks of doing what you've done. I've always believed that if something is meant to be, it will be. But, what do I know?"

"Mathew, I'm not usually one to beg, but I will. I'll get down on one knee, I'll say 'please' a million times over. I'll sign any wavers you print up so you are not held responsible for anything that happens." I was begging. I knew it and I didn't care.

"Daniel, can you let me think about this overnight?" Mathew asked. "I will promise that I will give the matter my complete consideration and will let you know in the morning of my decision. I would like to go over all my notes and figures of prior research. I would like everything fresh in my mind before I agree. Can you entertain my request and keep patient until morning?"

Steve Wilhelm's: Another Time To Love

"I guess, if I have no other choice," I said. "You've always been cool with me before. Well the other you's have. Okay then." I stood up. "It won't be easy, but I will do my best to keep myself occupied until the morning." Call Megan and talk to her, I told myself. That will keep you occupied.

"Very good, Daniel. I will call you first thing in the morning."

"If you do decide in favor of moving ahead, is it something we can do tomorrow as well?" I asked, hoping, praying.

"Let's play that hand when it gets dealt, shall we?" Mathew reached out his hand.

We shook and I left. I was not dejected, but I was not elated either. I just had to keep thinking positive that Mathew will decide to help me.

***

The next morning, I took a shower after getting the coffee maker brewing. As I was unplugging my cell phone from the charger, I noticed I had a missed call. My heart raced as I hoped it was Mathew. However, the caller ID said it had been Megan and she'd left a message. I hesitated before listening to it. Was it the guilt of me wanting to leave that made me pause? I couldn't take Megan with me. I couldn't undo Lizzie's death. I didn't like the way I was handling things, but if I had been given the

Steve Wilhelm's: Another Time To Love

'fight or flight' option, I was choosing flight. I pressed the message prompt to hear what Megan left for me.

"Daddy, I'm sorry I haven't been answering your calls. I have been coping the best way I know how right now. I know you wouldn't approve, but I've been partying and things pretty much every day. Anything to get my mind off of Mom being gone. I'm okay, really. Please don't worry about me. I just have to deal with this in my own way, right or wrong. I know that sounds selfish, but it is what it is. And if anyone could understand that, I know you will. I won't overdo it, I promise. I will stop if I think I'm starting to lose control. I'll be strong, just like you, Daddy. You'll be okay until I'm able to get back home to be with you. I love you, Daddy. Bye."

I didn't know what to think of her message. I listened to it twice more, and each time, I wished Megan was here so I could wrap her up in my arms and tell her everything was going to be okay. I would tell her that I am so proud of her and that someday I wish I could be as strong and intelligent as she is. At the same time, I sensed she didn't want that. She wanted to be left alone. I have to respect that of her. I believe her when she says she'd know when to stop partying. I think she might be surprised to find me sober right now, under the circumstances, but she would be extremely disappointed to know I was only that way because I will be escaping back to the last timeline I just came from. At least that's what I was hoping would happen.

Steve Wilhelm's: Another Time To Love

I poured myself some coffee and went out on the patio to sit and contemplate. I really wanted to phone Mathew and see if he'd made a decision, but I didn't want to pressure him. He said he'd call, and for me to be patient. I took a sip of coffee and my cell rang. I spilled the hot liquid in my lap as I reached for the phone. Fuck, that was hot, I thought. I answered without looking at who the caller was.

"Hello?" I said.

"Daniel, this is Mathew. I've decided to go ahead and work with you. Can you be at my office in a half hour?"

"Yes," I almost yelled into the phone. "Of course I can. Thank you, Mathew, you have no idea how much this means to me!"

I jumped out of the lawn chair and ran inside to change pants. In less than half an hour later, I was walking into Mathew's office feeling much better about things than I had been. He took me into the back where the bed and all the necessary equipment to perform the procedure were located. It was all the same as I remembered from both times. He had me lay down on the bed.

"Okay, Daniel," Mathew said. "I would imagine you are the pro in this, so I don't need to tell you too much." He put the electrodes on my chest and arms and then the metal band on my head. He pulled the syringe out of his lap coat pocket and pressed the plunger in until all the air was released.

Steve Wilhelm's: Another Time To Love

"That almost looks bigger than the last one," I commented.

"Unfortunately, I wouldn't know," Mathew said. "It's the one I have that has the latest serum I developed."

"To help facilitate activity in the region of the brain that will help in the 'travel,' yes I remember."

"Indeed," Mathew nodded. "Perhaps I could use you as my assistant if this doesn't work out."

"Don't take this the wrong way, Doc," I said. "But, I hope that's not something I will need to consider. This has got to work."

"Might I remind you of the possible damage your brain might suffer in doing this, Daniel? There is still time to reconsider, you understand." Mathew reached behind the computer monitor and pulled out a clipboard.

"I appreciate that," I said. "I really do. This is something I have to do. Believe me. I know the risks, but I think this will be the last time. One way or the other, I think when I get back, I'm there to stay. I'll have a lot of things to work out, relationships to smooth over. I'll be digging in with both feet. At least I know everyone I love will still be there." That's what I hoped.

"Fair enough," Mathew said. He held the clipboard in front of me and handed me a pen. "I just need you to sign this. It states you are willingly and with full consent participating in this procedure. You acknowledge the risks involved and understand that I will not be held responsible for any of the consequences that could occur

Steve Wilhelm's: Another Time To Love

that we've talked about. I'm not saying anything will, but this is just formality, of course."

"No worries," I said. I signed the form and he put the clipboard back behind the monitor.

"Are you ready for the injection?"

"Plunge away," I answered.

"This might sting a bit, it's a larger than the average needle."

"Plunge away," I repeated.

Mathew injected me and I felt the familiar warmth spreading throughout my body. As before, my cares and fears disappeared and grogginess overcame me. It was very pleasant. He departed into the back room to monitor me through the window. The music began playing in the background and I closed my eyes. I thought about Lizzie, Jules, Maggie, Jeff and Mom. About how much I wanted to see them all again. I concentrated on being back, being back, being . . . then there was darkness.

I heard music. It was the same peaceful, calming music I heard right before I blanked out. I opened my eyes and saw I had not gone anywhere. I was still in the bed in Mathew's office. Damnit! It didn't work. Mathew suddenly appeared by the edge of the bed, a frantic, worried expression on his face.

"Daniel, are you all right?" he asked. "There was a major spike in your brainwave activity just now that has me extremely concerned."

"I . . . I'm okay," I said. "Very thirsty, though."

Steve Wilhelm's: Another Time To Love

He left the room briefly and came back with a cup of water with a straw. He held it next to my lips for me. I sucked on the straw and took some of the cool liquid into my mouth. That's better, I thought as I swallowed gingerly and it tasted so sweet and good.

"Easy, Daniel," Mathew said.

I moved to sit up and that's when my head began to pound. It felt like a concrete jackhammer was being used to break into my skull. I lay back down and the pain subsided a bit.

"Fuck, man," I said and winced. "What the hell is wrong with me? Is this what you were warning me about?"

"What do you mean?" Mathew looked slightly confused.

"You just told me right before you injected the solution into my arm that I was risking brain injury by the excessive 'travel attempts.' I took the risk and if I'd gone back, it would have been okay. But it looks like it failed, because here I am."

"It is true I had concerns," Mathew said as he removed the headband and looked at the readings on the monitor. "But we hadn't discussed them yet."

"What?" I was now confused. "How long was I out this time?"

"Not very long," Mathew answered, "I believe not more than ten minutes. All the readings were normal and then suddenly the readings began to fluctuate until they were pegging way too high. If you hadn't regained

Steve Wilhelm's: Another Time To Love

consciousness by yourself, I was going to give you a manual shock to bring you out myself." He walked back into the room behind the two way mirror and came back with another syringe. "Allow me to give you this for your pain. It's a mild pain reliever that will dull your headache, but won't put you out."

I nodded my head. I was okay with anything that might bring me some kind of reprieve from the agony coursing through my head. He injected the contents of the syringe and a moment later, it felt as if a layer of insulation was placed all over the inside of my head. I could feel the pressure of the pounding, but it was merely a faint reminder of what I had experienced just minutes before. I was able to sit up with very little discomfort now.

"I don't know what's in that concoction, Mathew," I said with a grin, "but I definitely think it would be in your best interest to market that shit."

"I'm more concerned about you at the moment," Mathew commented. "Can you tell me what you experienced after you lost consciousness?"

"There was nothing," I said. "I had been concentrating intensely on coming back to before you sent me back, and the last thing I was aware of was the music. Then, the first thing I was aware of was the music. But, you don't remember telling me about the danger to my brain with repeated attempts? You had me sign a waiver, dismissing you of culpability should anything happen."

Steve Wilhelm's: Another Time To Love

"This is fascinating, Daniel," Mathew said. "I did not have you sign anything before we began the procedure."

"What?" I didn't understand. "You put the clipboard right behind the monitor after I signed it."

Mathew went to the monitor and turned the cart so I could see all sides. There was no clipboard. "I'm sorry, Daniel. Perhaps you just need some rest before we figure out our game plan. You should go home and relax, let the brain rest."

"Maybe you're right," I said.

"I wouldn't recommend driving until after the pain medication wears down a bit. You could call your daughter and she could give you a ride."

"Megan?" I was confused. "I don't know why you would suggest that. She's in New York and I doubt I'd be able to talk to her. She's God knows where, 'grieving' her mother's death."

"I don't understand," Mathew looked at me curiously. "You told me you had just had coffee with her before coming to see me. Her name is Maggie, isn't it?"

I swung my legs over the side of the bed. Goosebumps were rising all over my body. Could it be? "Are you fucking with me now? I mean, no offense, but I think we're talking about two different timelines. Did we not just run into each other at the tavern for the first time yesterday?"

"No, I met you Friday when I'd come back from my trip to Portland."

Steve Wilhelm's: Another Time To Love

"Holy Shit!" I exclaimed. "I think it worked! I'm back!"

I pulled the electrodes off of my chest and arms stood up from the bed. I was just about to reach for Mathew's hand to give him a congratulatory shake when it felt like a fireworks factory had exploded in my head. My knees buckled and I sank to the floor, holding my head in my hands. Mathew helped me back up on the bed and I lay back down, resting my head on the pillow.

"No, I don't think you are going anywhere for a bit," he told me.

"How about another shot of that pain shit," I suggested, my words echoing loudly in my head. "Maybe the first shot wasn't quite enough."

"I could give you a stronger dose, but that would be pushing it. I don't know the extent of the damage you have suffered." Mathew left the room once more.

Every little move I made felt like needles were being shoved deep inside my head. Even blinking my eyes caused me to wince. What good was coming back if I wasn't able to do anything? Mathew had to come up with something. I wasn't going to go through another procedure, I had already decided that. I just needed to be well so that I was able to start making amends in this reality and get my life back together. Was that asking too much? Mathew came back into the room.

"I'm going to be okay, aren't I?" I asked.

He took the top off the new syringe he had brought with him and cleared the excess air. "This should help

Steve Wilhelm's: Another Time To Love

more," he said. "I can't risk giving you anything more without looking over the readings from the procedure." He injected the contents and once again, the pain dulled to a mute roar.

"Thank you," I said gratefully. "I can function better now."

"Stay here for a while," Mathew said. "I'm going to be in the other room going over the information I have." And with that, he left the room.

I faded in and out of clarity and had no idea of the present. It was somewhat like being on mushrooms, but without the feeling of helplessness. It was a nice little trip, I thought.

After a while, I realized that I had to pee. My bladder felt as if it was stretched to the limit. I looked around the room and couldn't see or hear any activity, other than the sound of the music from the hidden speakers.

"Mathew?" I said out loud. "Are you still going over the readings?" No answer. Tentatively I moved my legs over the side and slowly stood, holding onto the bedframe to keep me steady. My head stayed clear this time. This was a good sign.

I walked to the doorway of the back room and peered around the corner. How much time had gone by since the last shot? The room was empty. Mathew must have gone out for whatever reason, I thought. I looked and found my jacket draped over the end of the bed and put it on.

Steve Wilhelm's: Another Time To Love

Reaching in to the pocket, I found my phone. I looked at the time and was amazed that only two hours had passed since I had gotten here. I smirked. Two hours. Time was irrelevant to me anymore. I had experienced two days in that few minutes I had been out of it when Mathew had sent me back. I pushed aside that thought, as I was sure it would make my head explode trying to understand the unexplainable.

I opened the contacts on the phone and found Maggie's name. I swiped to the right to place the call.

"Hi Daddy," she answered. "Are you done with the doctor?"

"Yes, I think everything's in order for now," I said. "Are you still nearby?"

"I'm just at the bookstore near the diner we were at." Maggie replied. "I was looking for books on pregnancy and what I can expect for the next nine months. Do you have time for lunch? I'm starving."

"Sure," I said. "That's a good idea. You have any place in mind you want to eat at?"

"Let's go back to the diner. I think I saw a great special on the reader board when we were there earlier. Does that sound okay with you?"

"Sure," I agreed. "I'll be leaving here in a few minutes. I'll meet you there."

"Love you, Daddy," Maggie said and hung up.

I put my shoes on and laced them up. I didn't know where Mathew had gone, or when he'd be back, but I needed to leave. I was feeling a lot better and my head

Steve Wilhelm's: Another Time To Love

was clear. Perhaps the last dose of pain medication did the trick. I went into the back room again and found a pad of paper. I wrote Mathew a note that I was leaving and would contact him this afternoon and let him know how I was. I then left his office and went down to the sidewalk.

It was overcast with a slight breeze, but it still felt good to take in the fresh air. It was a wonderful contrast to the stale air inside the office. I started to make my way to meet Maggie at the diner. I had walked a block and then felt a pulsing inside my head. Damn, the headache had returned. I saw a bench at the bus stop just ahead and sat down. I just needed a few minutes to see if the ache would go away. Maybe I just needed some food. That was probably it. I had experienced headaches before when my blood sugar level had been low. That would explain things, I thought. I got up and started walking again.

I turned the corner and saw the diner on the other side of the street. Maggie was standing outside near the front door. She looked up and saw me. A big smile appeared on her face and she waved. I waved back and made my way into the street. Halfway to the other side, I was literally blinded by an immense white light that flashed behind my eyes, followed by a crippling pain that shot through my body. I stumbled to my knees and cried out. I heard a shout, it was Maggie, then a scream. I opened my eyes to a squint and saw her face contorted in fear. She was pointing behind me. I managed to turn my head and saw the front grille of a Toyota Sienna hurtling

Steve Wilhelm's: Another Time To Love

towards me. There was the screeching sound of brakes and tires on the road.

The next thing I knew, I was on the edge of the sidewalk. I couldn't feel my arms or legs. Maggie was kneeling over me, one hand was on my cheek, the other I could feel stroking my hair.

"Oh, Daddy," she said, looking at me tenderly, tears were streaming down her cheeks. "You're going to be fine."

I took a breath and it felt like I was sucking in razor blades. Something was very wrong with me. "Jesus," I gasped. "I don't think I'm going to be fine. I . . . can't feel anything." I tried to move my head so I could look at my body, but even that slight attempt at movement was denied by my body.

"Daddy, don't move," Maggie said. "I've called nine one one, just hang on, okay?"

I'd never felt so weak before, I felt like I had zero energy. I felt something run down my cheek from my forehead. Maggie reached her hand down and wiped with the sleeve of her shirt. I could see that it was blood, as the sleeve now had streaks of red on it when she pulled away. "Maggie," I whispered. "I need to tell you something."

Maggie leaned her head down and tilted her ear close to my mouth. "I really think you should save your strength, Daddy," she said.

"I don't think I have much time left," I said slowly. "I really need you to know what I've done, what I've caused."

Steve Wilhelm's: Another Time To Love

"*Shh,*" Maggie put a finger on my lips.

"No," I managed to shake my head slightly. "Maggie, I love you. I am so proud of you. I hope you keep the baby and if it's a boy, name him after me, so he can be my namesake. I just think you need to know what I've done, so you maybe can understand why I've been so troubled." It was so hard to talk, but I had to get everything off of chest.

"Daddy, you're not going to die on me, don't you dare even consider that," Maggie cried. "Besides, Mom would kill you."

"Just listen to me," I said. "Please?"

"Okay, but once the ambulance gets here, you'll be fine. They'll get you to the hospital and they'll take good care of you, you'll see."

I told Maggie everything. I didn't think she'd believe any of what I told her, but I hoped that she might consider the possibility of what I did. I knew it to be true. I told her that Jeff understood and grandma did too, so she could always talk to them.

Maggie watched my face carefully through my admission and maybe she was just being polite or the loving daughter, but I didn't see any signs of mistrust. I heard sirens in the background, but instead of getting louder, they were fading in my mind.

"Daddy!" Maggie yelled at me, her face filling with anger.

"Maggie?" I whispered hoarsely. The edges of my vision were fading into gray. My eyes wanted to close.

Steve Wilhelm's: Another Time To Love

"Daddy, don't you fucking leave me!!" I heard Maggie screaming, but it was as if from the other side of the street, not right in front of me.

"Maggie . . . please tell your mother . . . I'm sorry and that I love her . . . more than she'll ever know." It was so painful to speak. "I . . . I love you . . . Mags. Take care . . . of yourself and the baby." The strength to even keep my eyes open was rapidly waning. I closed them. I felt Maggie's lips kiss my cheek. She cradled my head in her arms and wailed. "I'm . . . so . . . sorry," I managed and then I let blackness overcome me. There was only peace and silence.

Steve Wilhelm's: Another Time To Love

Epilogue

"Daddy!! Please don't leave me!!" I screamed at his face. His eyes had closed and there was no movement behind them. I put my hand on his chest and could not feel a heartbeat. I put my ear in the place my hand was and listened intently. There was nothing. No heartbeat, nothing.

The medics had arrived and they gently pulled me off of Daddy. "Let us do our thing, now," one of them said.

A Kirkland police officer came over to me to ask me questions on the accident. It was all starting to blur together. Somehow, I made it through the interrogation.

"It all happened so fast," I told him. "Daddy was crossing the street so we could go into the diner and have lunch. He suddenly looked to be intense pain, and fell to his knees. He never saw the car coming towards him. I don't know that the driver saw Daddy until it was too late. It was as if the impact happened in slow motion. The car hit Daddy and he was thrown to the sidewalk just in front of me. I don't remember what happened to the car, all I know is Daddy was laying in front of me, bruised and crumpled. He was talking to me and then he . . ." I couldn't go on.

The officer wrote down everything I said in his notepad and then gave me his business card, saying he would be in touch. The medics put Daddy in the

Steve Wilhelm's: Another Time To Love

ambulance and told me they were taking him to Overlake Hospital and I should go there as soon as I could. I nodded and told them I would. Mom needed to know what happened. I called her and it went to voicemail. I left her a message to call me about Daddy. Another officer came over and asked if I needed a ride anywhere, or if there was anything she could do for me. I said thank you, no. I was unable to cry anymore, it seemed all my tears were gone.

    I needed to call Grandma and tell her about Daddy, but there was something I had to do first. I squinted my eyes as the sun bore into them, and turned in the direction of Mathew's office.

Steve Wilhelm's: Another Time To Love

Another Time For Maggie

Prologue

My name is Maggie Allen. I'm a college student attending New York University. I'm from a good family from the Seattle area. My parents were married for over 25 years and were both very successful in their careers. My father, Daniel, recently passed away from a random, brutal accident. It devastated everyone. I am going to get him back.

Steve Wilhelm's: Another Time To Love

CHAPTER ONE

The services for Daddy were emotional for everyone that came – a relatively small group of people that were mostly family members. A handful of his associates from his job including his boss and immediate members of the team he worked with showed up. Everyone was gracious with their words and memories of Daddy. It made me feel good that he was appreciated. I miss Daddy more than I could say.

I will never ever forget that day. Having to see Daddy being hit by the car, and then watching him die in my arms, was probably the hardest thing I will ever have to go through. No child should ever have to endure that kind of thing.

I have decided that I will keep the baby I'm carrying. If it's a boy, I will name him Daniel, at Daddy's dying request. I had originally planned on giving the baby up for adoption, but things change. And we adapt. We have no choice. But after listening to Daddy's last words to me, I'm thinking we do have a choice.

Daddy had a choice. He just acted on it incorrectly, but that's my opinion, based on the way things played out, and his own admission. We'll see if I make the right choices. Sometimes we do the things we have to do, that we believe is right. I'm going to keep my fingers crossed.

Steve Wilhelm's: Another Time To Love

Before I was able to get ahold of Mom and Grandma the afternoon of Daddy's death, I went to see the doctor he had been to that morning. From what Daddy had told me, I wanted to meet this Mathew. Not to accuse him of causing the accident, but to see if he could help me the same way he had helped Daddy. I had put myself together as best I could and went to Mathew's office. I walked in and he happened to be sitting at his receptionist's desk, looking intently at the computer monitor. He looked up as I entered the office.

"Good afternoon, is there something I can help you with?" He asked me.

"You are Dr. Mathew Stevens?" I asked. I knew he probably was, but I was being polite. I needed him to be on my side.

"Yes, I am," Mathew answered. "And you are . . .?"

"I'm Maggie Allen. You knew my father, Daniel."

"Knew?" Mathew looked at me, then at the computer screen. "Oh, God, please don't tell me he's the victim in the accident on the news."

"Unfortunately, he is," I said.

"I am so very sorry for your loss," Mathew said. "Your father was a good man."

"Thank you," I said. "I appreciate that."

"I'm shocked," Mathew commented. "He was just here a few hours ago. Can you tell me what happened?"

"He was meeting me for lunch," I started to explain. "He was just starting to cross the street, and then something happened. He told me it felt like something

Steve Wilhelm's: Another Time To Love

exploded in his brain and he went down. He was halfway across the street when it happened. He never saw the car that hit him."

"I was afraid of something like that," Mathew said.

"I need you to tell me everything about what you and Daddy were doing, what he was involved in."

"I'm not sure that would be ethical," Mathew said. "There's a confidentiality clause that all doctors have with their patients."

"You'll have to pardon my language," I said, "but fuck the doctor-patient confidential crap. I'm his daughter. He's dead. And I need to know what exactly he was doing. I mean, he told me, but he was dying as he was telling me. So I want to hear it from you."

"Of course," Mathew said. "I suppose that under the circumstances, I can share some things with you. Can I ask you what you're intention is with the information?"

"If everything he has told me is true, then I want you to send me back so I can stop him from being in the accident. I want to prevent his death."

"I'm not so sure that would be a good idea," Mathew commented. "I tried to tell your father about the risks of changing that which has happened. Things occur for a reason."

"I think there's a bit of a difference between what Daddy did and what I mean to do. Going back as far as he did, of course anything he changes will have ripple effects all up the line to the future. I just want to go back one

Steve Wilhelm's: Another Time To Love

day, and save him. There is no future that will be affected. How could anything I do cause issues?"

Mathew invited me into his consultation room and he told me about his and Daddy's history. It corroborated what Daddy had told me, which, if I had had any doubts before, they were now dispelled. Mathew asked me questions about my health and if I had any heart issues, or high blood pressure, anything that might cause me danger should he perform this procedure on me. I of course said no to those things. It was evident Daddy hadn't told him about my pregnancy, as I was pretty sure that would sway Mathew's consideration of my request. I wasn't going to bring the fact up myself. I was more than willing to take the risk if it meant saving Daddy. I love my baby, but I love my Daddy too. I need him in my life. Hell, Mom needs him too. So does Grandma.

Mathew asked if I would consent to him taking blood samples and performing a physical.

"Did you do that with Daddy before you treated him?" I asked.

"Fair question," Mathew said. "No, and that was a mistake which I don't intend to make a second time. It might have made a difference. But I can't change what has happened."

"No, that's my mission, now." I said. "What all do you check for in the blood test," I asked, curious, thinking about the pregnancy.

"It's nothing too invasive," Mathew told me. "I'll check your red and white blood cell count, do a metabolic panel

Steve Wilhelm's: Another Time To Love

test, blood glucose and cholesterol levels, that sort of thing. Would there be anything specific you would like me to test for?"

"No, no," I said. "I was just wondering. I'll give you consent for the test."

Mathew performed the physical and told me he would be in touch with me before the end of next week. I was anxious to begin as soon as possible, but Mathew wanted to be on top of everything before starting any procedure with me. He wanted to make sure I was healthy enough to tolerate the impacts to the heart and brain. Mathew said as long as all my readings were within specifics, he would have no issues working with me on my mission.

I thanked Mathew for his time and discretion. I gave him my cell phone number and then left. It was time to start notifying everyone about Daddy's death.

Stay tuned for more of Maggie's story. Coming Soon!

Made in the USA
San Bernardino, CA
04 August 2017